My King's Palace

My King's Palace

RIYA AND RANI

PARTRIDGE
A Penguin Random House Company

To order additional copies of this book, contact
Partridge India
000 800 10062 62
www.partridgepublishing.com/india
orders.india@partridgepublishing.com

Contents

Inspired by Rabindranath Tagore, Satyajit Ray, and Rituparno Ghosh

Thank You R, R, A and A for reading my stories and believing in me

The Rag Doll

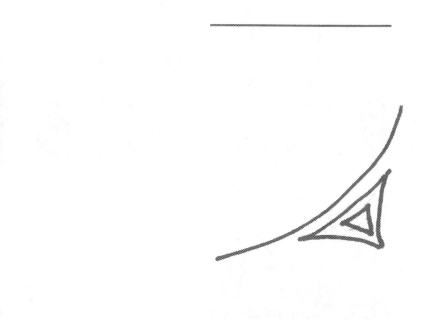

Everything went black. A wave of disorientation swept over her as she tried to focus on the surroundings shaded in monotone. Her eyes were blinded by streaks of light like those penetrating, burning through a tattered curtain. It was a light that did not radiate luminosity, but one that scorched her innocence. Everything faded and then came into dim focus.

She turned around, trying to make sense of what was happening. She was gasping. She stumbled in the muddy field, desperately trying to feel something. She could not. Her hands felt numb.

She suddenly heard a shriek behind her, and almost immediately, a voice started ringing in her head, clamouring to break out. It urged her to run, run like there was no tomorrow.

She screamed her lungs out, 'Run, Puto, run.'

She ran. She ran until she was out of breath, until the world around her started spinning, until she had left everything behind her. She stopped when she realised she had left behind everything.

+ + + + + + + + + + + + + +

She turned slowly, very confusedly, trying hard to figure out where she was and why she was there. Then slowly it came back to her. She was with Nikhil in the evening when she had a bad cramp. She felt empty, somehow, and hollow.

'Where was Hiya? Was she OK? Was everything fine? Why was nobody around her? Why was it so silent?' she wondered.

Then she realised it was Nikhil standing by her bed. His eyes were sunken, and his face was as expressionless as a blank page. He slowly pulled her hand into his and began to gently caress her hands, as he always did when he wished to comfort her. She stared back at him. He whispered in a barely audible voice and an apologetic tone, 'I am sorry.'

She tried hard to gather herself. 'Sorry, but why? About what?' She thought, 'Wasn't it more likely for them to talk about Hiya now? Did she resemble Tapati or was it Nikhil?'

Then it gradually dawned on her. She realised that maybe that is what Nikhil was struggling hard to tell her. Hiya never made it. The gynaecological complication, which the doctor had warned her about, had finally taken its toll. Hiya was lost. Suddenly everything around her was surrounded by a mist as translucent as a shroud. She was back in the muddy field, once again, all alone, She wanted to scream out, 'Hiya, where are you? Don't be afraid. I am coming.' Yet all she could manage was an agonizing groan.

She saw the statues of half-forgotten dreams attired in grey looming over her stillborn daughter. With her eyes shut firmly, she tried to look at the world through Hiya's eyes, hoping to find a light that may outshine her despair. Long and ever-stretching were the hallways of darkness where no light could survive. It took her by her arms and engulfed her.

When she woke up again, Nikhil was sitting beside her, his dark brown eyes like a murky ocean after a tempest. Nothing seemed to make sense to her, nothing at all.

+ + + + + + + + + + + + + +

Nikhil did not know what he should be more concerned about, losing Hiya or losing Tapu (that's how Tapati was called in her family). For Tapu was lost. His first thoughts were to be with her immediately after he heard about Hiya. But somehow Tapati was not there. She did not cry; she did not even say a word after she learnt about Hiya. It seemed as if she was somehow rendered absolutely incommunicado. Her soul was lost is an ever-spinning vortex of guilt and anguish, a never-ending tunnel that led nowhere.

Nikhil had to sign the papers for the last rites of the daughter that they had been anticipating for months. Hiya's face was about as pale as Tapati's now. Her eyelashes were long, just like Tapati's. But she would never open her eyes and behold this world. 'What a waste,' he thought. It terrified him to hold her; she was cold and frail yet so beautiful.

He wanted to cry with his wife, but it seemed that tears had dried up for them both. Hiya was conceived within two weeks of Tapati's viral pox, and the doctor had warned them about a complication that may arise. He had suggested an abortion. Tapati had vehemently campaigned against abortion. She said she had unknowingly betrayed someone once in her life. She had promised herself that she was not going to betray ever again. Nikhil could never understand what betrayal she was referring to. He asked, but Tapati would not tell him. She only said that it was very private and that it hurt her even today to remember. Only after Hiya completed eight months and was kicking away in glory had they hoped that the worst was over.

Nikhil was concerned about Tapati's health. She seemed to have sunk down an abyss so deep that nothing or no one, not even Nikhil, could reach her. When Nikhil had proposed to Tapati, she had asked him, 'What did you see in me?'

'Your eyes, Tapati,' he had told her. 'Your eyes are a reflection of your mind. When you're happy, your eyes light up everything around you, true to your name.'

'When I am sad?' she had asked.

'It's an eclipse, Tapati. As if Rahu—the demon—has overshadowed your mind.'

Now it was neither. It was as if something within Tapati had died. Something had scarred her, beyond repair. It was as if she never had a soul.

+ + + + + + + + + + + + + + +

Nilima called, 'Tapu, Tapu, where are you?'

'Ma, I am, I am, here on the window sill.'

'Why don't you go out and play, Tapu?'

'I don't have friends, Ma.'

'OK, then, make friends.' She paused. 'You have so many nice toys. Why don't you play with them?'

'I don't like them, Ma. They are all dumb toys.'

'Why don't you play with the soft doll that your uncle gave you?'

Tapati still remembered how it all started. Not only did she start playing with the doll, but she named it Puto. It was hardly a doll. It was more like a little baby-shaped plastic face wrapped in soft cotton. It was unlike the conventional hard plastic dolls with false eyelashes and coloured lips. It was soft, almost human, with a dimpled smile and cute eyes. It was a rag doll. Puto became her first friend. Wherever she used to go, whatever she used to do, Puto was always with her. She used to have conversations with Puto. She would tell Puto about her school; she would tell her about her teachers, her classmates, and her secrets. She used to hold on to Puto and hide when her parents used to quarrel. Puto was her friend; Puto was her confidant. In some way, Puto was also her little baby girl.

Tapu slept with Puto. Puto had a couple of clothes which Tapati would change for her regularly. Puto even used to get a weekly bath, with Nilima's favourite soap, much to the chagrin of Nilima. Whenever Puto was out of sight, she would call out for her. 'Puto, Puto, where are you?' It was as if Puto was a real person, who could hear and respond. Puto was more real to Tapati than anyone else in the world.

+ + + + + + + + + + + + + +

Nikhil did not know what to do, and after much discussion within the family, it was decided that it would be best for them to take a short vacation at Tapati's parents' home. She had not been there for a long time because of her pregnancy and subsequent complications around it. Nikhil thought that it might help Tapati to get back to normal life.

After Barun's retirement, Tapati's parents had shifted back to their ancestral place in Jamshedpur. Tapu had spent a good part of her childhood there while her father was away in Punjab, a particularly difficult posting during those days of heightened Sikh terrorism. Her grandfather's place in Jamshedpur gave Tapu her first taste of freedom. There were huge fields with lots of trees; there were secret rooms up in the attic, full of her grandfather's collection of old records and books. Her favourite was a deserted balcony in the back, full of discarded material and junk that was supposed to be thrown off but never was.

+ + + + + + + + + + + + + +

Every day, she and Puto would go for a new adventure. Some days it would be in the middle of the field, inhaling the smell of wilderness, wandering off like Maria and children of *Sound of Music*. Some other days, they would explore the fields with her grandfather's binoculars. She looked forward to coming back home from school to the comfort of Puto's soft arms and vibrant face.

Around that time, Tapati became friends with Bubai. Bubai was the lonely recluse who lived across Tapati's grandfather's place. His parents would always be arguing over something or the other. On days that were less noisy, it was worse, and there was more violence. When drunk and angry, Bubai's father did not even spare him. His only friends were his books, which he read and reread till the pages came out of the seams. Tapati followed Bubai with binoculars and came to sympathise with him. She was the one who reached out to him.

'Why don't you come out and play?' she asked.

Bubai had found it hard to conceal his smile. He answered, 'Would you play with me?'

'Yes, I would.'

'What's your name?'

'Tapati, Tapu.'

'Aren't you afraid that I would engulf you like Rahu engulfs the Sun during solar eclipse?'

Tapati had considered the tall, lanky frame of Bubai, smiled, and said 'No, I am not afraid. The Sun's spirit is indomitable. Solar eclipse is only temporary and that too very rare. Tapati is the daughter of Sun. What makes you think she would be any different?' she demanded.

'Oh! You know a lot for someone so young!' Bubai was amused.

'Yes, my mother told me,' she had declared proudly.

He loved to listen to Tapati as she chatted away on trivial matters of the world. He would at times borrow

Tapu's binoculars and watch Tapati and Puto as they went about their new adventures. Sometimes, he himself would be part of those adventures.

Bubai once asked, 'How can you go on talking to Puto for hours together? It is, after all, a one-sided conversation.'

Tapu answered, 'No, it is not one-sided.' She paused and added,

'You have to have special powers to appreciate her.'

He said, 'You know, I like how "Puto" is part of "Putol"—the Bengali word for a doll.'

Tapati smiled. She already liked Bubai. She liked the way he made her feel special.

'Also a clever arrangement of alphabets makes the name sound like an anagram of Tapu.'

'Yes, not everybody gets it,' she smiled again.

'You must love Puto a lot. To give your doll a name that is practically an anagram of your own name.'

Slowly, Bubai and Tapati developed a strange bond between themselves. In spite of their age difference and all other differences, they developed a sense of camaraderie. On days that were bad, Tapati understood Bubai's pain without him sharing it in so many words. Bubai was slowly filling up the time that used to be solely reserved for Puto.

It was late monsoon. Barun had come on leave for two weeks. Tapati's playtime had reduced as she was busy trying to soak in her father's warmth as much as possible. She knew he had to return to his posting in Punjab. Tapati would snuggle up to him soon after she was back from school. He seemed to be the only person after Bubai who really understood what Puto meant to her. On that fateful evening of 7 August 1991, Tapati had gone out in the evening for her usual playtime with Bubai and Puto, having missed it for a couple of days. Tapati wanted to return early as Barun had promised to take her for a drive around Subarnarekha. She only went because she did not want to miss the sweet pickle that she and Bubai used to have every Wednesday. She looked dazzling in the pretty red and yellow Punjabi bhangra dress that Barun had got for her. She was all set for her first motorcycle ride. When she did not return on time, Barun and Nilima were concerned, but they assumed that she was stuck somewhere, waiting for the rain to subside. When she did not return even after the rain subsided, Barun got worried, gathered a search party, and went looking for her.

They searched for her in all directions and called out her name, yet there was no response. Finally, Barun found Tapati under a banyan tree, her hair in a mess, her face strewn with tears and dirt. Tapati was running a high fever and had no recollection of the evening. Barun picked up the unconscious body of Tapati, gathered her carefully in his arms, and took her home. He did not notice that Puto was missing.

Only when Tapati opened her eyes and asked for Puto he realised that his daughter's constant companion was missing. Barun wanted to go out and search for Puto just like he had searched for Tapati. However, it was late in the night, and the weather was not good. Tapati was shattered when she realised that Puto was missing. She cried bitterly and did not want to sleep. Barun picked up Tapati's frail form in his arms and took her around, her head on his shoulders, as he tried to sing lullabies and make her sleep. Eventually, in the wee hours of the morning, Tapati slept.

When Barun went out into the fields the next morning, Puto was there in the mud with one of her hands missing and also one of her eyes. The rats in the field had taken her to be some sort of food and had gnawed into her before they lost interest and left Puto to rot in the field. Tapu was inconsolable. Somewhere in her subconscious she held herself responsible for Puto's suffering and death.

Nilima and Barun made sure that the mangled remains of Puto were properly cremated so that Tapati could have a closure. They had planned to give her a proper send-off by immersing her ashes in the Subarnarekha River. But Tapati refused to part with the ashes. The ashes were put inside a rosewood box with intricate inlay work depicting an elephant. Tapati kept the rosewood box on her bedside table along with other titbits and jealously guarded it at all times.

Tapati was traumatised beyond healing. Neighbours suggested that Barun should take her to psychiatrists, who were considered to be 'doctors of mad people' by some people in those times. Some malicious neighbours even suggested that Tapati was physically abused that evening. More than anything else, Puto's loss haunted Tapati for a long time in her nightmares. She would wake up in the middle of the field every night, with Puto calling out for her help to fight off demons gnawing at Puto. Barun had to extend his leave to take care of Tapati. Almost every night she would wake up from her nightmare, crying out in desperation, 'Run, Puto, run.' Every night, Barun would embrace her and cuddle her to sleep again. He would then console her and tell her how Puto, being a Hindu, would get reincarnated and would be born again. Puto was not lost forever. Slowly, the nightmares stopped, and in about six months' time, everything returned to normalcy.

+ + + + + + + + + + + + + +

Tapati came back to Jamshedpur to her roots. Nilima was always on her side. Nilima had hoped that the ambience of the place would relax Tapati and help her recuperate. But it did not seem to work. It seemed as if the world had stopped for Tapati. She never talked about Hiya, never cried or reacted. It was as if she was living in a time warp, waiting to be woken up by the touch of magic.

During the day, she would curl up in the easy chair on the balcony with a blank expression on her face. Only sometimes at night she would wake up and scream in her sleep. She had betrayed Puto. She had again betrayed Hiya. Hiya was her one chance of redemption. And she had lost it.

Barun and Nilima were at a loss. They finally called Nikhil and asked him to come down and spend time with Tapati. Maybe a husband's love could heal what a mother's care could not.

Nikhil started taking Tapati out for walks in the mornings and afternoons along Subarnarekha every day. He would chat away, more of a monologue, while they sat together on the banks of Subarnarekha. Even Nikhil was slowly losing hope. He did not know this Tapati—what she had become.

That afternoon, a funeral party had come down at Subarnarekha. It was an elderly couple. They had lost their only son in an accident. They had come to immerse his ashes in the Subarnarekha. The father said aloud, 'Bubai, my son. May your soul rest in peace.' Nikhil noticed that Tapati was paying attention to their rituals. It was the first time she had paid attention to anything after Hiya's loss.

Nikhil turned towards her and told her in his deep, sedate voice, 'You know, Tapu, I think Hiya would like to come back to you someday. But you have to give her the chance.'

Tapati was thinking of Bubai. As memories flashed by, slowly she also remembered how events had unfolded on that summer evening, the evening she lost Puto. It was as if she was retrieving a long-repressed memory from somewhere deep in her past, so dark and so deep that it seemed unreal. The face of an old, forgotten acquaintance flashed in front of her; it was Bubai's face. She remembered that Bubai was trying to impress her with some new science stuff that they had been taught at school. She remembered waiting for the street vendor who used to sell sweet and sour pickles.

She remembered the naughty glint in Bubai's eye when he said that he could get her something really sweet, something that he had learnt in his science class, something that was a combination of potassium iodide (KI) and two molecules of sulphur (SS). She remembered his tall, lanky figure looming over her. For one moment, she had felt cornered, nervous. That was when he kissed her. He kissed her first on her cheeks. Tapati was too shocked to react. He looked into her eyes and misjudged her confusion for consent. He then kissed her on her mouth. She pushed Bubai away, his burning lips scorching her skin. Tapu felt a dizziness overcoming her, a sickness arising from her stomach. She wanted to throw up then and there, but she was suddenly conscious of Puto. She could feel a blinding rage rushing through her veins, subdued only by a terrible fear of Bubai and overflowing concern for Puto. She held Puto tightly to her chest and broke into a run.

She ran. Deafening silence mounted in layers over her, as the walls closed in. She was running through the narrow hallways of darkness. Every leap away from Bubai still seemed much too close to him for her. Every passing second engraved it deeper in her memory that she had been defiled. With every beat, her heart pumped blood into her arteries, blood which was impure. She felt violated. She could almost hear somebody urging her on, 'Run, Tapu, run.' She ran and ran. The rain lashed against her bare back as silent tears trickled down her cheeks. She ran through the fields with Puto in one hand, as if she was trying to get away from herself, away from all that had happened. She stumbled in the muddy fields, and her pretty red-and-yellow dress was torn by thorny shrubs. Yet, she did not stop. She ran as if there was no tomorrow.

Now, she realised for the first time that she had not betrayed Puto. She had been betrayed by Bubai. Hiya's death was not her fault. She wanted to tell Nikhil all about Puto, all about her first betrayal, something that had been repressed inside her for so long. She remembered how Barun and Nilima had wanted to strew the ashes of Puto on the banks of Subarnarekha. She then remembered the rosewood box. Puto's ashes were still there. She had not given a proper farewell to Puto.

She turned to Nikhil and told him, 'Nikhil, I want to go home. Please take me home now.'

'Yes, Tapu. It is better to go home. It is going to rain.'

'No, Nikhil. I need to do something. It is urgent, Nikhil. It is long overdue.'

As soon as she reached home, she ran inside and asked Nilima, 'Ma, Ma, I need the rosewood box.'

'Now?' she asked.

'It is time, now,' she added. Nilima had preserved the rosewood box with Puto's remains all these years. She opened her safe and silently handed over the box to her daughter.

'Nikhil, please take me back to Subarnarekha.'
'It is going to rain, Tapu.'
'Please, Nikhil.' There was a sense of urgency in her voice.

When she reached Subarnarekha, she took out the rosewood box with the elephant inlay work on top. She opened the box and slowly placed it on the water. She was finally ready to give her Puto a proper farewell. It was raining. She could smell the earth, feel the pain oozing out of the earth as the rain quenched its thirst and mended its parched soul.

'Come back to me, Puto,' she said in an inaudible voice. 'I will be waiting . . . ,' she added.

Tapati then narrated the story to a perplexed Nikhil as the rain drenched her completely. It washed away all the dirt, all the malice of the nine-year-old Tapati. As she narrated the story to Nikhil, she knew that she had to get better and get back to life. She had to do it for Nikhil, for Puto, and for Hiya. She knew Puto was waiting to come back to her warm embrace, waiting to come back to Tapati again. As the clouds dispersed and the sun slowly revealed itself, through the rain, for the first time after Hiya passed away, Tapati had a reason to live, a reason to love.

The Homecoming

Sujoy was in a tearing hurry. It felt as if his entire life was slipping through his fingers like sands of time. He was practically sprinting through the narrow lane of his ancestral North Calcutta home, something that could possibly have been normal at San Francisco, which he called home now. But it was definitely weird in the narrow stretch of Kasi Bose Lane. There were no taxis around. It was very difficult to get taxis in the early morning. Most of the lot would be gone for an airport drop or pickup. The ones that were still plying the streets would have spent the night with the halogen lights of Calcutta. And as the rude sunlight pulled the magical veil off the face of the city, the taxi drivers rushed back home. He ran like his life depended on it.

He practically jumped into the first yellow taxi that he could get hold of. He urged the taxi driver, 'Please drive fast. I have to reach the PG hospital soon.'

Sujoy stared out of the window. A big red communist party flag was on display on the junction of four roads. A red hammer, sickle, and star on a stark white background glared back at Sujoy. The Communist Party of India still ruled West Bengal. A through and through anti-communist, a through and through believer of the capitalist philosophy, Sujoy would have reacted adversely to this loud display of communist symbol, even yesterday. Today, it did not matter to him. He could see the kaleidoscope of his life playing out in front of his eyes in black and white, as if in slow motion. He had to reach the hospital before it was too late.

+ + + + + + + + + + + + + +

Sujoy was coming back home after ten long years. When he went to America—the land of opportunities, the land of capitalism—he was a bitter yet ambitious young man full of dreams, daring to take on the world. At the time of leaving, Sujoy had vowed that he would never come back to Calcutta, never to set foot on a communist land ever again in this lifetime.

Sujoy loved Calcutta. It was much more than a city to him. It was his home, his world—the narrow lanes of North Calcutta, the smell of *Tele bhaja* (fried veggies), the shops selling oversized T-shirts at throwaway prices, the honking of the taxis, the *tring-tring* ringing of the tram bells. Even now, when he closed his eyes and thought of Calcutta, he could feel it all coming back. Then he could hear his mother calling out 'Tutun'—his nickname. Calcutta reminded Sujoy of everything he loved. Most of all, Calcutta reminded him of his mother, Shefali, who had been his world. It also reminded him of his father—Subhomoy.

+ + + + + + + + + + + + + +

Subhomoy was a professor of physics. He used to carry a strange sloppy, shapeless, strapped bag on his shoulders every day when he went to the university. His hair would be dishevelled, and his crumpled shirt would be partly tucked into his trousers. He could never remember to wear the shirt Sujoy's mother had ironed for him. Only his moustache was done up in a way that gave him a stern, forbidding look. With his dishevelled hair and stern moustache, he looked almost comical from certain angles. He could never remember any of the household chores that Shefali asked him to do. But he never forgot to attend the party meetings. He attended them without fail and believed that communism would bring equality in society. He believed that he would be a messiah to the downtrodden masses against the bourgeois. Sujoy remembered the party members blocking roads as marched away and chanted at the top of their voice:

'Down with the black hands of the bourgeois
Break them, grind them,
Break them, grind them'.

They would chant with their lungs bursting out—as if people's lives depended on it—as they walked past the meandering roads of North Calcutta, in front of Sujoy's home. To Sujoy, they seemed like religious sermons in continuous monotonous rhythm, only much more aggressive. It was strange, as the Communists were atheists. The procession would have men in their cheap cotton shirts, their hair plaited with oil. They looked all serious, wearing casual sandals instead of shoes. The women in the procession would be characterised by their simple printed cotton saris that they wrapped around with a casual carelessness. They were so unlike Sujoy's mother, who would wear her sari in perfect plaits, and even after a hard day's work, the plaits would be exactly in place. In the sweaty hot afternoons of Calcutta summer, when everybody smelt of sweat, a sweet smell of sandalwood would exude from her, a smell that would always remind Sujoy of his home and, more importantly, his mother.

When the people in the procession were done, they would stop at Bhola's tea shop for the occasional cup of tea which would be sweetened to the core and tasted like sweet syrup. It would be accompanied at times by triangular fries, stuffed with vegetables and potatoes, though mostly it would be just potatoes loaded with spicy chilly. They would burp after having the fries due to indigestion and acidity developed through years of untimely and unhealthy food habits.

Sujoy was fascinated by these processions but was never able to understand them. He wondered why the men cried hoarse against America and wanted to break the black hand of America. It seemed as if America was some sort of a monster, waiting to gobble up all men. As he grew up, he understood that America was a country and so was China. He had once asked his father if India was a part of China, all because he had heard the demonstrators chant 'China's chairman is our chairman', which he had found very strange just after learning in his geography class that China and India were two different countries. He had been tempted to ask his geography teacher the same question but had refrained from doing so.

His father's glasses were heavy. He was the university topper in physics. He had decided to stay on in his homeland instead of leaving for the greener pastures of America like his bourgeois friends, who ranked much lower than him and had much limited intellectual ability. He had dreamt of 'revolution'; he had dreamt of a country free from the shackles of poverty. Though initially appreciated, it had not gone down well with Sujoy's grandfather, Sridhar, who had even told Sujoy so, when he was old enough to understand. As Sridhar sat sprawled on his easy chair on the terrace, smoking a hookah—an old multi-stemmed contraption for smoking tobacco—he often told Sujoy that it was the love of communism that had destroyed the beautiful mind of Subhomoy. Long after, Sujoy realised that beautiful mind or not, his father loved Lenin, someone he had never seen in flesh and blood, much more than he loved his family. And it had hurt Sujoy, more than anything else. He had felt anger, resentment, and then frustration against this character of Lenin, which later on turned to extreme apathy towards his father.

Shefali was as unlike Subhomoy as possible. She was always a picture of poise and composure. Her forehead smeared with red vermilion, her face always curved out in a smile. Sujoy's friends used to tell him that she exactly resembled the idol of goddess Durga that they worshipped every year. She embodied the softness of a pampering mother and the sternness of a goddess. Shefali was a graduate in mathematics with honours—in the age when it was not unusual for most women to get married at a young age and stop studying altogether. Sridhar had liked her intelligence as much as her pleasing personality and had arranged Shefali's marriage with Subhomoy. Shefali always remained very dear to him. Sridhar was closer to Shefali than he could ever be to his son, Subhomoy. He would profusely tell everyone who cared to listen how he had known her to be his saviour the very first day he had gone to their home to select a bride for Subhomoy. In private at times, however, he regretted his decision, not because Shefali had any shortcomings, but because he believed that Subhomoy could never be the husband that Shefali deserved.

Subhomoy seemed like a forlorn figure at home, almost as if he was a guest, almost as if he had lost his way and had landed up at Wonderland. He would suffer in silence, or may be just have a smoke, as Shefali and Sujoy would go about attending their plants with great energy. He would nod his head in a dispassionate, almost mechanical, way as an exuberated Sujoy told him about the first flower in his Chrysanthemum. It seemed as if he had been hijacked or transported on a time machine to a different time and space. He looked at the world like a bystander, perplexed by its curious ways, trying to fathom them in vain. Sujoy had seen him excited about anything other than politics and communism on rare occasions only. It was just about *Sarat*—the Bengali season declaring the going away of the monsoon rains and the advent of festivities of Durga Puja. Sujoy and his mother had planted a night-flowering jasmine tree. Subhomoy had discovered the small white flowers with orange stems covering the ground, when he had gone for his regular morning walk. He had been beside himself with joy. He had collected the flowers and put them in a bowl with water. He had taken care to add a tablet of Crocin so that the flowers remain fresh for a prolonged period of time. He had put it up with care on Shefali's Kashmiri curio side table in their bedroom.

Sridhar would wait for his Shefali to serve him food every afternoon. After which they would chat about the world at large, while they went about news items in the newspaper, chewing sweet beetle leaves rolled into a triangular shape with *paan masala* and cloves. At times, Sridhar would reminisce and share anecdotes from the past, and Shefali would listen, her hand on her cheeks, mesmerised with Sridhar's narrations. They would talk about every possible topic, but they would never discuss Subhomoy.

On the terrace, Sridhar would be on his easy chair half inclined, his eyes half closed, and Shefali would be on a Kashmiri floor mat, with intricate embroidery. They would savour every minute of each other's company. Shefali loved to bask in Sridhar's fatherly warmth. Sujoy had never seen his father as comfortable with Sridhar as Shefali was. Shefali was an embodiment of cheerfulness. Sujoy had only seen her wipe her eyes with the end of her sari, secretly, as his father conveniently forgot to keep his promises—promise of being there on Sujoy's birthday, promise of being there as she performed Saraswati Puja (goddess of education) and Lakshmi Puja (goddess of wealth) painstakingly, promise of being there at Sujoy's violin performance. Sujoy could never understand what hurt his mother more, the continuous sufferance or his father's silent nonchalance towards her.

+ + + + + + + + + + + + + + +

Sujoy's train of thoughts was broken by the pilot's announcement that they would shortly be landing at Calcutta. Sujoy could feel his throat choke and a strange knot in his stomach. He would be back in the city he had left with a lot of bitterness. It was his favourite city. Yet he had promised not to be back here.

Sujoy spent the next twenty-odd minutes in a sort of trance as the plane finally landed at Calcutta. It was raining outside, a slow drizzle, in the morning itself. He could smell the raindrops on the parched summer fields; he could hear the sound of soft drizzle. It was almost like a dream. All that seemed missing was his mother's rendition of Tagore in her sweet, mellifluous voice, as she strummed lazily on her sitar, oblivious of the world.

He could hardly recognise Runu Auntie after so many years. She oddly seemed very different from her vivacious self of ten years back; only her smile remained the same. For the first time, Sujoy noticed that Runu Auntie had the same eyes as his father. Her eyes were dark, brooding, and yet they had a strange sparkle to them. Sujoy would have never come to Calcutta. It was only because Runu Auntie convinced him to be there. Runu Auntie had called about a week back to inform him that Subhomoy was not keeping well. It was six o'clock in the morning for Sujoy.

'Tutun—Runu *Pishi* here. How are you?'

Sujoy answered, 'Yes, Auntie. I am fine. Is Uncle OK?'

'Yes, I called about your father.'

There was an uncomfortable silence for a couple of seconds. Then Sujoy asked, 'Did you really call me to talk about my father, after all that transpired?'

'Tutun—please listen to me, will you?'

'What is it Runu Auntie?'

'Tutun, it is complicated. Can you please come, Tutun?' There was a pregnant pause . . .

Sujoy asked, 'Why me, Runu Auntie? Why now?' He paused. 'Runu Auntie . . . I will bear all the expenses, as usual. Do not worry about it.'

'Tutun—this time it is serious, Tutun. Please come.'

Sujoy protested, 'Auntie, I cannot.'

'Tutun, your father has cancer. Please come.' She paused. 'Tutun, I think your mother would have liked you to be here at this time,' she said desperately.

Sujoy's head exploded. How dare she take his mother's name? Who was there with him when he held his mother's lifeless body and rocked it like he was putting a little baby to sleep? Then he realised . . .

'Did you say cancer?'

'Yes, Tutun.' She continued, 'Tutun, I know there are certain pains that even time cannot heal. But if you do not come, how different will you be from your father?'

Sujoy did not want to be like his father, not in this respect.

'OK, I will come,' he said. He would never do what his father had done. Never, ever!

+ + + + + + + + + + + + + +

It was 1991.

Shefali had not taken Sridhar's death in 1989 too well. It hurt her somewhere deep down. She did not just lose a father-in-law; she lost a friend. She missed their afternoons together. She stopped having her favourite sweet beetle leaves. She even stopped cooking *moori ghanto*, a delicious connotation of fish head with oriental spices, which was a favourite of Sridhar's.

Subhomoy also had not taken his father's death well, or so it seemed. Sujoy wondered whether it was his father's loss or his irritation at a Gorbachev doing away with policies of Subhomoy's favourite Communist Party of Russia. He remembered his father arguing madly with his friends in his room staffed with Russian literature and books on communism. He remembered his father professing that 'with communism gone, the world will be guided by greed and greed only'. His father was particularly concerned about the renewal of the Union Treaty, which was due in 1991. To Subhomoy, the world was falling apart.

In March 1991 Estonia, Latvia, and Lithuania declared independence. It represented a major threat to the Soviet Union's territorial integrity. In the 17 March referendum on 'the preservation of the Union of Soviet Socialist Republics as a renewed federation of sovereign republics', six republics—the three Baltic republics and Armenia, Georgia, and Moldavia—did not participate, and in April, Georgia followed the Baltic republics' example by declaring itself independent.

In April 1991, the Warsaw Pact, which had bound Eastern Europe militarily to the Soviet Union for thirty-five years, was formally liquidated. Gorbachev, the Russian President, did nothing to prevent all this. Subhomoy was livid.

'Gorbachev and his deputies must reinstate the structure of Communist Party to ensure that all the republics continue together in the new union,' said Subhomoy, trying to make everybody, who cared, understand.

'The entire Soviet Union will collapse otherwise! And America will become the single largest power in the world, a power guided by capitalism, a power guided by greed.'

He really was a visionary, as future events would turn out. However, what he would fail to notice was the shift of balance of power towards America in his own home front.

His son listened to Beatles and dreamt of travelling to America to make his dreams come true. He had cleared his SAT exams with high scores, and he was seriously considering them. Shefali knew all about it. Subhomoy had no clue.

It was 1991. It was on 18 August that Gorbachev was held virtually a prisoner; the State Committee ordered tanks and other military vehicles into the streets of the capital and announced on television that they had to take action because Gorbachev was ill and incapacitated.

On 23rd August, Sujoy came back home and found his mother in bed, down with fever. She was running a very high temperature. She still recognised him.
'Tutun, your grandfather is calling. I must go.'

Sujoy called Runu Auntie, as he trembled all over. Runu Auntie got Dr Sen, their family physician, immediately.

'It seems to be malaria,' Dr Sen said. 'How many days is she having this fever?'

Nobody knew. Shefali never told anyone.

Sujoy sat beside his mother's bed in constant vigil. Subhomoy had gone for an important party meeting to take stock of these events. He was not even aware that his wife was critically ill. It was Natabar, their help, who was only a couple of years older than Sujoy, who had held it for Sujoy.

'Are you there, Subho?'

'It's me, Ma.' Sujoy's voice choked.

'Subho, can you run your fingers through my hair? You used to do it so well.'

'Yes, Ma.' Sujoy could barely reply. She was still looking for the Subhomoy who had married her and brought her home, a Subhomoy who was caring and responsible, not yet a true comrade.

As she felt his teardrops, she whispered, 'Don't you worry, dear. I will be fine.'

Sujoy held his mother close as he ran his fingers through her silky hair and dozed off.

On the morning of 25th August, when Sujoy woke up, Shefali was really fine. It seemed she was resting after a long day. There was a smile in the corner of her face. She looked happy. Only, she was cold. She had passed away during the night, peacefully, in Sujoy's embrace. Sujoy could not even understand when it all happened. He was stupefied as he held the stone-cold body of his mother in his lap.

'Tutun, we are not been able to reach your father anywhere.'

Sujoy stared blankly at Runu Auntie.

'Tutun, we have to cremate your mother. It is getting late,' she said.

By 25th August, the leaders of the coup had given up; Gorbachev came back to Russian Parliament and was humiliated by Boris Yeltsin. Gorbachev had to reluctantly agree to Yeltsin's plan of dissolution of the Communist Party. The party was held responsible for the coup. Gorbachev resigned as the party's general secretary. The Communist Party of Russia, Lenin's dream child, had ceased to exist. So had Shefali.

When Subhomoy came back home, he found his family mourning for the departed soul of his wife, Shefali. Only he did not have any part in it. He wanted to console his son, but he was so far away that he dared not reach out to him.

Subhomoy forgot he was a communist and followed all the Hindu rituals for the deceased. He even sacrificed his hair, even his moustache, though technically, as a husband, he had little to do in the last rites of his wife; the main responsibility was the son's.

On the thirteenth day, after Shefali's Shradha ceremony was over and the relatives had left, Subhomoy went to talk to his son.

Sujoy was in his room.
'Tutun,' he called.
Sujoy turned, his stare cold.
'Tutun, I . . . ,' Subhomoy faltered.
'Baba, I have decided to go to America to complete my studies.'
'But, Tutun . . . ,' Subhomoy again faltered.
'Everything is already planned . . . Ma knew about this.'
'But, Tutun . . . you cannot . . . It is a lot of money.'
Sujoy looked directly at his father. 'You do not have to worry about it. I have full scholarship. You are free now

to devote time to communism and Lenin,' he had added sarcastically.

Subhomoy had felt the floor sliding away under him. He had sat down on the bed, holding the corner post of the bed, completely stunned.

Sujoy was in Calcutta for the couple of months, planning for his travel, mourning his mother, or sometimes chatting with Natabar. He never talked to his father. When he needed to tell something to his father, he asked Natabar to carry the message. Natabar was the bridge between them. Sujoy left for America within three months of his mother's death. He never came back to Calcutta.

+ + + + + + + + + + + + + +

Sujoy was not married. So all it meant was convincing his boss that he needed to take a month off. His boss, Robert, was very surprised. Sujoy had never talked about his family with his colleagues. He was the guy from India, who loved hiking, who always tried to convince everyone that Salt Lake City in Utah was exactly like Purulia back in India. He loved books and, most importantly, hated communism in general and hated Lenin in particular.

Robert asked Sujoy, 'Are you OK?'
Sujoy replied, 'Yes, I am fine. But I need to take off. It is a family emergency.'
Robert could understand that Sujoy did not want to pursue the subject and dropped it. His leave was granted. He just asked him, 'You will be back, right?'
At last Sujoy smiled. His boss was a caring individual. He came forward, shook hands, and in a deep voice, said, 'Yes, I will be back. Where will I be if not here?'

Now Sujoy was at the Calcutta International Airport, which was exactly as it was when he had left for the States. The world had moved on, Calcutta, apparently, had not.

Sujoy touched Runu Auntie's feet, as is the Bengali custom of greeting elders. He could hardly recognise Ashok, Runu Auntie's son, as he pulled up Sujoy's suitcase.

As they travelled in the car, Runu Auntie told him that his father was in a very painful state. He was suffering a lot. In his delirium, he often called out to his 'Shefali' and 'Tutun'. Runu Auntie went on rambling.

Sujoy hardly listened. He was inhaling all that was Calcutta—the stalls on the roadside serving morning tea, the lonely tram that trotted along like a prehistoric animal that has lost its way. As the yellow taxi pulled up on their street, Sujoy could hardly believe his eyes. The palatial premise of his ancestral home had been reduced to ruins at places. Time had taken its toll. The giant structure was still standing strong, but one could see its vulnerabilities. The place in the middle of the courtyard, where his mother used to light up candles as she played the conch shells and prayed to God every evening, was covered with weeds. It was very desolate. Strangely, the window of his mother's room was open.

'That is the room where Subho moved into after he was diagnosed with colon cancer, about three months back.' Runu Auntie detected his surprise and informed him.

'It is vacant now, after he had to be shifted to hospital.'

Sujoy was too stunned to say anything. He nodded.

'Did he . . .' He paused; plucking up enough courage, he asked, 'Did he ask for me?'

'No, he knows you only too well. He begged me not to tell you anything about his suffering.'

'But of course, when he is in pain, in his delirium, he often calls you.' She paused as if she was hiding something.

'What?' asked Sujoy.

'Every time he talks to you, in his delirium, he asks for forgiveness.'

Sujoy had wanted to run as far away from his father as possible. He had rarely thought about his father during his long stay abroad, without a tinge of bitterness and anger. Every day, as he shaved in the morning, Sujoy looked at himself in the mirror, and the tall, lanky frame of Subhomoy stared right back at him. He hated it. The only difference from Subhomoy was that Sujoy's shirt was usually pressed and properly tucked into the trousers, and his hair was impeccably brushed back. It was a saving grace that unlike his father Sujoy was clean-shaven. He had often wondered how he would look if he too grew a moustache like his father. Would he be his father's mirror image? No way. They were as far apart as the North Pole and the South Pole. But weren't opposite poles supposed to attract? His mother, Shefali, used to say that there was a very thin line between love and hate, and only the best of friends could turn the worst of enemies. So was he in reality very much like his father? Was that why they repelled each other so much? Shefali was the only bridge that could ever bring them together. And it was her death that finally led Sujoy to severe all relationship with his father. That was a long time back. Yet it seemed like only yesterday. Sujoy suppressed a sigh as their old help Natabar started fussing over his luggage.

'Your room is right beside your father's current room.' Sujoy's trance was broken.

'He had stuffed his room with old trunks. All that the trunks have are old letters, books, and old clothes that belonged to Shefali and you. Your father knew that his time was running out.

'I have opened the room just beside Shefali's room for you to stay. I hope that is OK,' Runu Auntie said.

'Yes, it is.' Sujoy nodded.

They went to the Chittaranjan National Cancer Institute to visit his father. The nurse and attendants were very respectful.

'Professor Subhomoy Roy's son?' one of them asked.

'Yes,' said Sujoy.

'Your father is getting the best treatment possible. Please do not worry. We respect Professor Roy a lot. Everything that can be done to ease his pain will be done.'

Even though only two people were allowed inside, the waiting area was crowded with people. People from his university, neighbours, people whom he had helped in life, all sorts of people from all walks of life. Sujoy never knew that so many people loved and cared for his father. The only person Sujoy would have liked his father to take care of was his mother. Yet, Subhomoy was not even there during her last rites. Did he regret it ever?

'How is he doing today?' Sujoy asked the doctor in charge.

'Are you his son?'

'Yes.'

'He is better, but he is still in a lot of pain. We are trying to keep the pain under control with medication, as much as possible.'

'He should not suffer,' Sujoy found himself saying to the doctor.

Sujoy was surrounded by people on all sides; everybody was a part of his father's life sometime or the other. Sujoy was a little surprised and bit annoyed too. He had got used to the American way of life too much and did not particularly enjoy people's adulation or interest in his private life. After all, none of his friends in United States knew about his father. It had saved him from extreme embarrassment that people did not ask and probe, like they did here in India.

After a long day, he had an early dinner and retired early. He woke up in the middle of the night, his body clock still attuned to American daytime. He could not get back to sleep.

That was when he noticed his violin in his father's room, through the half-opened window. This room had been his mother's before. 'Why had his father moved there?' he wondered.

The door gave a feeble squeak as he slowly opened it. It sounded strange in the middle of the night, as if it was a sound from a distant past. The room was stacked with books. There was an old HMV record player, and there were many records. Some of them were recordings by his father, some old Bengali songs. His father loved folk songs and songs of Tagore. And there were letters, loads of them, letters to his father and letters from his father . . . to his mother.

Sujoy ignored the letters. It would be incorrect to probe what his father wrote to his mother about. He started playing his old violin. He was delighted to play it after so many years. It was as if something had been there within him, in an enchanted sleep, under the curse of the wicked fairy.

He put up an unmarked record. It was a recording of his mother's recital of part of 'Sesher Kobita'—the farewell song by Tagore.

All I have ever given you
Has been your gift only
The more you have received . . .
The more I have been indebted to you, my love
My dear friend, goodbye

'Shiuli, why "Sesher Kobita"?'
'I like it so much, Subho.'
'I do not. It is so sad. That is the trouble with Rabi Thakur. All his beautiful plays are tragic. It is always "Kach-o-Debjani".'

Sujoy could hardly believe that his father knew about so much about Tagore's literature, that too romantic literature.

He stopped playing the record. He picked up a letter, oblivious of the fact that he was intruding into private lives. It was his father's, dated 24 May 1972. He read as under:

Beloved Shiuli,

How are you? How is Tutun? I miss you so much. I miss Tutun so much.

When I think of him, I can hear his giggles. He has eyes just like yours, soft and caring.

In Moscow, it is summer now. Moscow summer is very pleasant, like winter in Calcutta. I was witness to a historic event of President Nixon's visit to Moscow. He was the first American president to visit Moscow. I hope with this America will give up its imperialistic habits, inspired by Great Britain, and stop the war in Vietnam. You must be wondering, why I fill my letters to you with all these political details.

You know, Shiuli, I want our son to be brought up in a free and fair environment, where everybody is equal. Not like the old zamindari system where my grandparents have ruled and the poor farmers have slogged and struggled lifelong. Not any more. We shall create a beautiful world where everybody is equal. That is my dream. I know, I have disappointed my father by not taking up a position in America after I topped in my university. But, Shiuli, I want to make amends to all the mistakes that my forefathers have made, and I want to be part of the revolution to create a beautiful and equal world.

Would you give me company? The path will be long and arduous. And without you, I shall never be able to achieve it. But you, me—we owe it to our Tutun, a world where all men are equal, a world 'Where the mind is without fear and the head is held high . . . Where knowledge is free . . . Where the world has not been broken up into fragments'.

I long to go back to Calcutta, to hold you and hold Tutun in my arms and feel your fragrance . . . .

It was early in the morning. Calcutta looked very different, enveloped in the golden rays of the rising sun. Sujoy suddenly felt restless. He wanted to go to the hospital right then. He wanted to hold his father. He wanted to know his father, once again, in a new light. He wanted to tell him how much he loved him.

When Runu Auntie woke up, she found Sujoy awake. He was pacing the room, fully attired.

'Runu Auntie, I have to go to the hospital, now.'
'Now? But . . .' She paused. Somewhere she knew Sujoy had to share a lot with his father. He had to share all that he had missed in the last ten years, all that they could have shared in their lifetime together, in their favourite city.
Sujoy said, 'I must go now, Runu Auntie.'
'Let me ask Natabar to call you a taxi from the main road.'
'No need. I will go by myself.'

That was when he started running through the narrow alley leading to their ancestral home in Kasi Bose Lane. He ran like his life depended on it.

He finally got a taxi on the main road. He practically jumped into it and urged the driver to hurry.

When he reached the hospital, it was hardly visiting hour. But everybody was sympathetic; after all, Professor Roy's son had travelled all across the globe to be with his father on his deathbed.

He felt awkward after rushing to the hospital. He looked at his father's frail frame. He sat down beside him and carefully held his hand.

He sat there holding his father's frail hands. He looked at his long fingers and remembered how he had helped him get his kite in the air the first time he flew his kite. He held the ball of string, bridle, and his father held the kite. With his heavy glasses and serious face, he had looked positively awkward. Even though he did not approve of kite flying much, he had been with Tutun the whole time and actually had seemed to enjoy his time.

His father stirred in his deep sleep.

He whispered to his father, 'I am here.'
'Who?' Subhomoy barely opened his eyes and asked.
'Tutun here, Baba'
'Tutun,' his father smiled.
'Yes, Baba.'
'I knew you would come, Tutun.'
'I came yesterday, Baba. I had been here, but you were sleeping.'
'No, no. I had been at the night-flowering jasmine tree, at the Shiuli tree, the one in the park.'
Sujoy wanted to stop his father. He wanted to hug his father's delicate frame through the intricate weave of channels and other wires. He wanted to tell his father how much he loved him and how sorry he was for not contacting him for so long. Instead, he pressed his father's frail hands within his own, and he forced himself to say, 'Jasmine tree? Which one?'
'The one that is there in the park? Your mother was there too.'
Sujoy remembered the tree and the orange-centred fragrant flowers that grew before the Puja. His mother loved to make garlands out of Shiuli and wear them in her hair.
'I was picking flowers for Shefali. I used to pick up Shiuli every morning and give it to her when she would come to play in the park with her friends.' His father continued, 'You know, "Shiuli" for my beloved Shefali.' He smiled mischievously at Tutun as if he was sharing a great secret.

'It was much before your grandfather formally arranged our marriage.'

Before Tutun could assimilate the knowledge, he added, 'She is my home. I am going home, Tutun.'

Then he stopped. There was a long pause. Sujoy was frightened. Had his father slipped into some sort of coma or delirium?

He ran out of the room, looking for the doctor at Emergency.

When he came back, Runu Auntie was sitting there, beside his father, weeping silently. She lifted her head and said, 'He's gone, Tutun.'

Sujoy knew that his father was not gone really; he was finally home, busy picking up night-flowering jasmines for his beloved Shiuli.

Immanuel

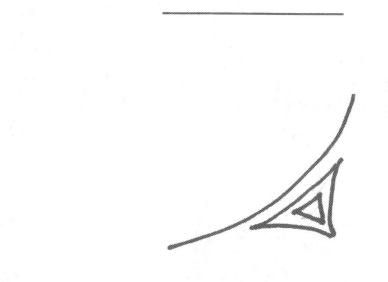

'Mama, I know how old are you.' Parama's heart skipped a bit.

But she had to ask. 'OK, dear, How old am I?'

'You are twenty years old!'

Parama was relieved at her son's innocence. She gave a big sloppy kiss, happily.

'No, Mamma,' Titun protested.

'Sorry?' said Parama.

'I am getting big. What will everybody say if they see you kissing me like this in the middle of a shopping mall? My friends can be here, you know!'

Parama smiled faintly. She was happy that her age still did not reflect on her face. Her son was only six years old, and he was already conscious. It was only a year or so back, when he loved to be cuddled, all the time.

She was draped in gorgeous red chiffon sari, and there was a round red sticker on her broad forehead; her diamond wedding ring flashed from her delicately framed fingers. Couple of years back, Parama would have found it extremely ridiculous if someone would have told her that she would be spending lazy afternoons out in a shopping mall, with her son, checking out shops and practically doing nothing. Yet here she was, looking at herself, her pretty hands looking exquisite in the blue and maroon combination bangles as they jingled and created a sort of melody every time she moved her hands. She was a little dusky by Bengali standards and had long flowing hair, which was frivolously left untied.

Yet she did not appear to be in particularly high spirits. She actually felt empty and vacant. Rajat, her husband, was busy at his office, in the middle of his myriad meetings that he had throughout the day.

Parama thought or rather she was certain that Rajat possibly talked more at office than at home. He was a forlorn figure at home, occasionally typing away on his BlackBerry—so much so that Parama reckoned his BlackBerry as more than unfair competition. Rajat was always too engrossed in his job, almost in love. He was, actually, too much in love with his work to notice other things around the world. He loved to succeed.

Rajat had given Parama a life of relative pleasure and relaxation, with servants to take care of their every need, do household chores, cook, wash, clean, look after Titun, and even perform the daily prayers. Parama had hardly any reason to complain. Yet somehow, Parama felt that she did not belong in the set-up; she was more like an extended guest. It was as if she on a ride in the luxurious train, *Palace on Wheels*, something she had watched on Discovery Channel. And when the train reached its destination, she would again resume her normal life. Parama felt that she led an almost useless existence. At times, in her dreams, she often saw this girl, her hair cropped in a bob cut, in bejewelled attire, pacing up and down the exquisitely designed train compartment, fervently asking co-passengers for her station.

Parama had learnt Hindustani classical music at Sangeet Research Academy under the guidance of famous vocalist Pandit Ajoy Chakraborty. She had wanted to be a playback singer. She had auditioned for singing in the film *The Morning Star* and had a fair chance of making it, when Rajat chose her instead. Theirs was a middle-class family, and her father did not want to let go of such an eligible bachelor like Rajat. She was married before she knew it. She had often pictured herself struggling to make it in the world of music; instead, she found herself in a gilded cage. Before she could settle down to her new life, Titun had come along. Parama's life became all about Titun. But life is a strange journey. The novelty of all good thing slowly fades away, even if it is the amazing feeling of holding your own flesh and blood in your arms. Parama showered all her love on Titun, so much so that any other women in Titun's life in future would find it difficult to win him away. Yet in spite of all this, a feeling of emptiness engulfed her from time to time. At times, she would be swept by a strange sadness, a longing for the path that she could have taken. She often wondered how her life would have unfolded if she had been able to carry on with her music instead.

Rajat had suggested that she join the digital bandwagon. He even proactively created a Facebook account for her and connected some of their close friends and relatives. Rajat had time and again suggested that she should start using the Facebook account so that she could be in touch with all her friends and relatives across the world. He possibly wanted her virtual friends and relatives to fill up the void that was created by Rajat's long working hours. He had hoped that it would make her happy. Parama used her Facebook account but not to the extent that Rajat would have liked her to. Rajat failed to understand Parama's sense of void. She would regularly visit her Facebook page to enquire about her friends, but she rarely had any new updates on her wall. She had nothing to share with the world. She felt positively claustrophobic in her Lake Road apartment.

Parama checked her watch. It was 4 p.m., time to return to the apartment and wait for Rajat to come home, not knowing if he would be there for dinner or not till it was too late to plan anything else. Her life was an eternal wait for Rajat to come home. However, today was Wednesday.

+ + + + + + + + + + + + + + +

Every week, on Wednesday, Parama would keep her ears wide open for piano renditions by Mr Gomes. Mr Gomes gave piano lessons to Jasmine. Every Wednesday, he would be there at 5 p.m. sharp. Jasmine was the only daughter of Marisa and Joseph. Joseph was a musician and Marisa a secretary in a multinational company. Joseph dreamt of making it big in music some day.

Parama once had the chance to take a peek into their apartment. It was mostly a bare apartment except for the baby grand piano, which seemed to take up more than half of the drawing room. The apartment was leased by Marisa's company, well known for its patronage of Anglo-Indian secretaries. The piano was an inheritance from Marisa's grandmother. Marisa was extremely proud of this possession. Marisa had listened to her grandmother's piano renditions in her childhood, when she used to play the instrument. Marisa had craved for this piano since her childhood days. Marisa's grandmother gifted this piano to her favourite granddaughter on her eighteenth birthday. Marisa was always full of stories about the piano. She treated it like a close family member. The piano was never even out of tune, even though the same could not be said about other things in their apartment, including the grandfather clock, which looked aristocratic but almost never showed accurate time.

The Wednesday piano lesson by Mr Gomes was Parama's escape route. She looked forward to every Wednesday. She imagined Mr Gomes's playfully moving his long slender fingers across the keyboard of the baby grand piano as mellifluous sounds filled the room and transported her to a different world.

+ + + + + + + + + + + + + + +

Parama got a little late in reaching her home. It was completely silent. She could not even hear a single piano note. Parama checked her mobile. She checked for the day and time. It was a Wednesday and it was fifteen minutes past 5 p.m. Yet she could not hear a single note of music.

She paced up and down her room. She was not sure if it would be appropriate to enquire about Mr Gomes. 'Has he come? Will he play the piano?' she wondered. She sipped her black coffee as she paced up and down. Finally, when she could not bear it, she knocked on their door.

When the door finally opened, everything was in a mess. And Marisa was sitting by the baby grand piano. Her slender, tiny frame was rendered smaller in comparison to the huge baby grand piano. Teardrops still lingered on her cheeks as she feebly smiled at Parama. Parama could not help but ask, 'Oh dear! What happened?'

Marisa stared at her blankly and informed her that Joseph had finally got a chance to play in a Bollywood movie music album and that Marisa had to quit her job at Calcutta and travel with him. Marisa and Jasmine had to leave Calcutta and all her relatives behind. Most importantly, she had to leave her baby grand piano behind, the very thought of which sapped away all strength from Marisa. Although Parama was shocked to hear this, she could not help but feel happy at the prospect that the piano might be up for sale. She would miss Mr Gomes lessons for Jasmine, but then again, she could start learning piano herself.

Even before Parama could think anything, Marisa held Parama's hand. 'Parama, I do not know anybody who can keep this baby safe. Can you do it?'

'Are you sure you want to leave the piano with me?'

'Parama, I do not know anybody else who will love it and keep it safe for me. I have seen you admire it with your eyes. I know you love music. I know you have enough space to keep it safe.'

'What more can I ask for?'

'Would you look after my baby for a year or so? We shall take it away, as soon as we settle down at Mumbai.'

Rajat objected vehemently. He complained that it would consume their entire living space. But Parama was absolutely determined to have it. She coaxed and cajoled Rajat and convinced him that having an old baby grand piano was like having an exquisite piece of antique. 'It adds to class.' She knew that if nothing, this would appeal to Rajat's sense of aristocracy. Parama even paid Marisa for the piano, in case they could not manage a big enough apartment in Mumbai to house a baby grand piano. For all practical purposes, she ensured that the baby grand was hers and hers only.

She even arranged her piano lessons with a lady teacher, who would come every week. She had wanted to learn from Mr Gomes, but she knew of Rajat's inherent dislike of men who spent time in jobs like playing a piano in general, and Mr Gomes in particular. Mr Gomes was a charmer and not the kind of man that Rajat would have liked Parama to spend time with.

She was so engrossed with her new possession that she forgot about her daily trips to the mall. Titun pestered her for a couple of days and then found an engaging hobby with Nintendo. Finally, after months of dedication, she graduated to Rabindra Sangeet on the piano. It was a hot sultry afternoon when Parama played her favourite Rabindra Sangeet, '*Choke Amer Trishna*'.

> My eyes are thirsty
> And thirst scorches my heart
> I am a rain starved sultry summer day
> my mind charred with repentance

Parama rediscovered 'Parama' after about eight years of marriage; she discovered the young Parama who was lost in the myriad mundane jobs of raising a child and been a good wife. In her pursuit of providing anchor to her family, she had lost herself somewhere. All her dreams, all her passions, everything that defined her had somehow been put to a deep slumber with the magical touch of the silver wand of the witch. Now that she was touched with the golden wand, she was alive once again.

She recited aloud Rabindranath Tagore's 'The Fountain Awakes' or '*Nirjhorer Sopnp Bhongo*'.

> How is it that this morning the sun's rays
> Enter my very heart!
> How comes it that early bird-song pierces
> Today the cavern's gloom!
> I do not know why, but after so very long my
> Soul is awake.

That night, she updated her status for the first time on Facebook. She wrote on her wall: 'Today I played Rabindra Sangeet on my piano . . . *Chokke amer Trishna* . . . *Trishna amer bokkho jure* . . . (My eyes are filled with thirst . . . And thirst scorches my heart) . . . '.

The first response was from Immanuel. She had only known him through her cousin brother, settled in America. Immanuel was a regular participant in the Bengali cultural meets in California. He liked her post and sent her a message: 'Dear Parama, . . . *Ogo bondhu* . . . *Ogo priyo* . . . *Majhe majhe praner pore poroskhani dio.*'

Parama had always considered this to be one of the most romantic poems of Tagore. 'Oh my friend, Oh my beloved . . . All I ask of you is to touch my heart . . . To touch my soul.'

It was long time since somebody had told Parama something so beautiful. Rajat never understood poetry, and it bothered him no end whenever Parama talked about poems. It had initially hurt Parama a lot, but over the time, she had learnt not to expect Rajat to understand poetry. As for Parama, her evenings were suddenly transformed, filled with music and meaning once again. It was as if she had travelled back in time, before her marriage, and found a friend that she could share her deepest thoughts with.

Rajat barely noticed it, though he was happy that finally Parama was engaged and self-contented. It also meant that he could spend more time on his X-Box Nintendo. Titun joined his father in his virtual sports pursuits. Parama never could make sense of it. If you really want to play, why not go out in the fresh air and play rather than getting stuck in this virtual world?

+ + + + + + + + + + + + + +

Parama's world was now full of her piano, her music, and of course, Immanuel—who inspired it all. She would stay up late into nights, as it was daytime for him, and catch up with her nap after Rajat left for office. She had never acknowledged Facebook to be a medium of communication. Yet there she was on Facebook every living night of her life.

Parama again learnt to admire what it meant to feel alive, what it meant to be passionate again, what it meant to be surrounded by music. Parama's life finally seemed to have the meaning that it had lacked. Her afternoon rendezvous stopped; her shopping spree stopped. She even stopped watching the mother-in-law and daughter-in-law serials on television. They seemed stupid and derogatory to all womenfolk. She, in fact, started pitying people who wasted their time watching those meaningless family dramas. Titun missed the sticky orange cone ice cream treats of the afternoon rendezvous. Parama started stocking them at home so that she did not have to go out in the afternoon with Titun. Titun did not complain, though having ice cream at the food court had a different kind of thrill. It was like a carnival, where you could watch interesting people and things as you lazily enjoyed orange ice cream cones. He missed the carnival, but the lure of Nintendo was stronger. However, he felt sad as somewhere deep down he had a strange feeling that he was losing ground. He kind of missed the way Parama would cuddle him and ask him about his day. He even missed her sloppy, wet kisses.

Parama was so engrossed with Immanuel that she lost count of reality and barely noticed anything else. Titun's school water bottle lay wasted on the floor till the maid finally figured out the problem. All her living hours revolved around Rabindranath, music, and Immanuel.

Immanuel's Facebook snaps clearly said that he was an extremely handsome man with a sensitive smile. He loved Tagore, Anjan Dutta (Bengali singer), and Beatles, so much so that his friends called him 'TAB'. It was a very interesting combination for a Jew, born and brought up in Kolkata. He called her 'Mon' which, in Bengali, meant 'my heart' or 'my mind'. She accepted that without ever asking how she could have been his heart when they had not met even once.

'You know, Immanuel, my father loved the colour blue, and his favourite god was Krishna.'

'That is fascinating.'

'Used to call me Krishnakali at times also . . . because I am a bit dusky.'

'*Krishnakali aami tarei boli* . . . To me you are the flower Krisnakali.'

'You know, Immanuel, you know too much about Rabindranath, considering that you are not even a Bengali.'

'Mon, I owe it to my father. He spent a long time at Rabindra Bharati, Santiniken.'

'Even I owe it to my father, you know. On my eleventh birthday, he had given me Rabindranath Tagore's *Khanika*. You know, Immanuel, it was marked "To my Krishnakali".'

'That's amazing. Mon, Do you really have dark gazelle-eyes like in Krishnakali?'

'Do I? It really depends on you. Beauty lies in the eyes of the beholder.'

'OK, Krishnakali, I will seek asylum in your gazelle-eyes.'

'You know, I had preserved the *Khanika* with a lot of care.'

'Then what happened?'

'I lost it, Immanuel, during moving, courtesy Rajat's job. It was as if I lost my father all over again.'

'Does Rajat know?'

'Not really, I never told him.'

'OK.' Immanuel wanted to write 'Why not', but he thought it might be crossing some sort of a line.

'You know what, Immanuel, I have still preserved my father's gramophone.'

'Really?'

'And the best part is, it still works fine. In fact, I have a couple of old LPs, mostly songs of Rabindranath Tagore.'

+ + + + + + + + + + + + + + +

It was early morning in September when Immanuel asked her, 'I have heard your melodious voice again and again as I replayed your songs on my VLCC player . . . Can I call to hear that beautiful voice? Will you talk to me, if I call you?'

Parama had never felt this way in her lifetime. She knew that if she agreed to take this call, this whip of wind had the potential to turn into a tempest, a storm that could blow her whole being away, yet she could not resist the temptation. She contemplated throughout the day. She tried to put her logical abilities forward. She even skipped Facebook for that night. The next morning, she could not resist any further.

She woke up from her sleep and logged in. It was 2 a.m. But Immanuel was not online. It was 3 a.m. in the morning when she dropped a message on Facebook to Immanuel, telling him that she would like to talk to him too. She even shared her mobile number. When he did not call by 5 a.m., she was completely distraught. She checked her mobile again and again.

When Rajat woke up, she excused herself, citing poor health, and locked herself in her bathroom. She cried like she had lost someone dear to her heart. It was 8 a.m. when the phone rang.

In a voice that cracked after her misadventure, she said, 'Hello.'

'Is that Parama? Immanuel here.'

There was a long pause after which she could hardly whisper, 'Yes.'

'I hope I did not wake you up. Did I?'

'No, not at all,' she laughed.

'Good. I have been waiting the entire day for this moment. Thinking when will it be morning for you.'

'And I was up whole night, thinking you would call me.'

That instant, by the touch of an invisible magic wand, they became something more than friends. Immanuel started calling her occasionally. Their conversations did not normally last long, but Parama would wait for his calls, just to hear his voice. The calls always left an indelible impression on Parama's mind.

One evening, Immanuel asked her, 'Mon (my heart), would we ever meet? Or will it be like "Priyo Bondhu" ("My Best Friend") of Anjan Dutta?'

Parama answered, 'There will be no exchange of letters for us. It will be only exchange of lyrics and songs.'

Immanuel paused and replied, 'Mon, there is nothing as eternal and as bright as love. It shines with its own light. You may not like to admit it, but you know and so do I.'

+ + + + + + + + + + + + + + +

It was a day before her birthday that Parama received a huge package by mail. Parama opened it find an original LP record, *The Voice of* Rabindranath Tagore *in Songs and Recitation*. It was an LP recorded by Rabindranath Tagore in his own voice. Parama could not contain her happiness. It had a recording of 'Krishnakali' too. The gift tag read, 'To my Krishnakali'.

That evening, Immanuel called her to wish her 'Happy Birthday' in advance.

'You should not get me such expensive gifts. I will get spoilt,' said Parama.

'I would love to pamper and spoil you. Did you like it?' Immanuel asked.

'I loved it, Immanuel. I have never ever received a more meaningful gift in my life.'

'You know, a large proportion of the recordings reproduced in this album was originally made in 1926 under the old mechanical process,' informed Immanuel. 'It will not perhaps possess the same quality of reproduction as current recordings,' he added.

'It's lovely to know that I own an LP with Tagore's voice on it.'

'Yes, it would possibly be considered to have some vintage, antiquity value. Mon, I am planning to come to Kolkata. I would like to meet you.'

Parama was totally stunned. Here was this stranger whom she had never met, yet he had the power to completely make her or destroy her. She had assumed that they would never meet in real life. Now he was there, coming to Kolkata to meet her.

She could barely whisper again, 'Yes.'

'I will come on the twentieth. Can I meet you?'

She could barely say yes again, and they decided to meet up at Victoria Memorial. 'Something to remind you of the times of Rabindranath Tagore.'

Parama could hardly believe her luck. She pinched herself hard to make sure that all this was not just a dream. She was so very excited that she hardly ate or slept. She was filled with this guilty happiness, somewhat akin to the feeling she had once, after she had finished the Lindt Chocolate bar, all by herself, without telling Rajat about it.

+ + + + + + + + + + + + + + +

Finally, 20 September presented itself. The sky was bright blue and the sweet sun shone through the array of white, spongy clouds. Parama got ready in a trance. She wore her favourite *basanti* (orange)-coloured sari. The sari draped around her like a flame of thousand passionate fires.

She arrived at Victoria Memorial ahead of time and was embarrassed at her own teenage syndrome. She loitered around Victoria Memorial for two hours alone, waiting for Immanuel. She even contemplated walking away from her appointment. But she stayed back.

She recognised Immanuel from a good distance. He looked exactly like his photos on Facebook. They walked through the lawns of Victoria Memorial. He was full of plans of going to Shantiniketan, walking on the banks of Kopai River, and visiting Rabindranath Tagore's Bishwa Bharati University. Parama agreed, not stopping to think that she had a family and just could not take off to Shantiniketan without giving rise to a lot of questions. Soon, Parama found herself in the embrace of Immanuel. He passionately kissed her. As she kissed him back, she thought it was wrong, yet she could not bring herself to end it, jolt herself out of this sweet surrender of love. Rajat hardly ever kissed her. And when he did, it was never so demanding, so passionate, so intense. Perhaps the illegitimacy of their relationship added to the excitement.

Just when they were lost in each other, they were rudely disturbed by the constable on duty, who castigated them for their immoral behaviour. Immanuel cowered down, lost his cool, and finally bribed the policeman. After the policeman let them scot free, he relented.

'We should have actually met at my hotel in private.'

'Only teenagers come to Victoria Memorial really.'

'Yes, it would have been costly possibly, but it would have been convenient too.' he went on

Parama listened in silence as the afternoon sun slowly went down on a poignant note. Parama saw Immanuel, for the first time, for who he actually was. He would stop at nothing to have what he craved. He would not stop to think before breaking another man's family or bribing a petty government official. He did not even have the decency to ask her if it would be possible for her to go to Shantiniketan all alone, given that she was married and also had a kid. He just assumed that she would leave everything behind and come with him at his beck and call. He had already made all arrangements. Everything was about him, about his convenience. For the first, she saw their relationship as it really was, a reflection of her idea of love and his idea of ownership. She suddenly remembered how she used to enjoy taking Titun out to the playground before all this.

She turned to Immanuel, looked directly into his eyes, and said, 'Possibly I had lost my way. I need to go home.'

Immanuel pulled his eyebrows together, unable to comprehend the change of situation.

Parama simply said, 'I have a son, Immanuel. He will be waiting for me.'

Immanuel's face grew dark with indignation, and his beautiful lips twitched involuntarily in disgust. He said, 'Oh!' and walked away as if he had never known her.

Parama returned home and sat down by her piano. She tried to play, but all that she heard was the faint sound of an out-of-tune piano cracking.

She was the 'Pygmalion' to her Immanuel. She had imagined him to be the man she always wanted to fall in love with and not the man he actually was. She was simply too much in love with the idea of being in love to see that.

Tears flowed down her cheeks as she sat on the stool about her piano, her sari carelessly flowing down her shoulders to the floor. She gathered her sari and draped it around herself. She then wiped her cheeks with the corner of her sari. She was a perfect poignant picture frozen in time.

It was then that Titun ran into the room and threw himself at her.

'You know, Ma, I am officially tired of Nintendo. Can you take me to the playground tomorrow? I would rather play there.'

Parama embraced her son and said, 'Yes, I will definitely take you there every day, starting tomorrow.' She hugged her son tightly.

A Child's Dream

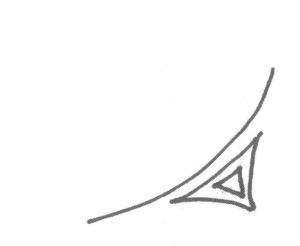

'So what do you want to be when you grow up?'

'I want be a princess.'

'I want to travel . . . the whole wide world.'

'I want to go to Hogwarts.'

'I want to build a city . . . with . . . Lego pieces.'

'I want to be happy.'

Our teacher had asked us this question. Now when I look back at all the answers and dreams, I realise that they could never happen. No one can be a princess unless one is Katherine Middleton. It's impossible to travel 'the whole wide world'. Hogwarts is an imaginary place, and it's useless waiting for a letter on your eleventh birthday. Believe me, I tried. Building a city with Lego pieces? One draught of air would topple it.

Happiness . . . is not a tender rose.

I am in my room.

Paulo Coelho says that when we really want something the entire universe conspires to make that dream come true. Ma says that there are only a very few dreams that we want to come true so desperately. Dreams are made of memories. Each man has a dream for himself. Does this mean that dreams separate people? One dreams of peace, another of war. One dreams of being together; the other feels that he is better off with someone else, even if it affects the one person he loves most, or so he claimed—his daughter, me. Ma wanted to stay with Dada. Dada did not want to stay with Ma. Sequences of unrelated images tumble in my mind. So many pieces of the giant jigsaw puzzle called life. I could try to glue the pieces back together and give them to Ma and watch her smile. I could be Matilda and she could be Miss Honey, and we could have delicious chocolates together. But that is what it is. It is my fantasy. I don't want to be a part of it any more. The reality is that Dada and Ma were together, and now they are not.

My eyes wander off to pictures of Ma and Dada, together, smiling and happy. So many cherished memories and smiles and counting our lucky stars. Then one day . . . snap. Quick and easy. Like tearing off a Band-Aid. At first, it feels like freedom and independence, and then the pain begins to settle. Then the scar, although not completely healed, appears, and we remember everything and it hurts.

Casper, my pet dog, scurries in my room. He always knows when I need him. Casper is lucky. He does not need to know that the two most important people in his life can't even look at each other, let alone be alone in the same room together. Dinners had become horrible. Just the clink of metal spoons used for serving. Other than that, it was just Ma occasionally asking me whether I wanted anything else. Then . . . silence—unwanted but given the circumstances, only appropriate. Dada did not let her serve. He didn't care that his little girl was watching him change so rapidly. Ma touched Dada's hand once. He pushed it aside. I pretended to ignore it. Am I able to express exactly how hopeless I felt at that moment? He is my father, and this is not what fathers do. Accidentally once, I spilt a little bit of water on the table. He was so furious. 'What are you doing? Is this what I have taught you? What a mess. Ask your mother to clean this up.' Ma was sitting opposite to me. I looked at her. She looked at Dada.

For my sake, Ma has endured him for a long time. The first breeze of unhappiness arrived three years ago when Dada invited a lady friend for dinner. I was eight. I liked her. She looked like she came from another world, a beautiful one. Ma was busy with work, but this lady would take me out to buy books and music CDs that my mother would never let me buy. She was the coolest person I had ever met, and I adored her until a few days ago when Ma mentioned her name while arguing with Dada.

Ma cries, even though very softly. Faint, occasional sobs. She is careful not to let me know that she is sad.

I once saw them while they were fighting. They were standing in two separate corners of the room. Ma was crying. I could see her tears, though her spectacles hid them nicely. Her jet-black hair, which cascaded down her shoulders, was in a mess. She fiddles with her hair when she is nervous. Dada was standing beside the dressing cabinet with his BlackBerry. He wasn't crying. I wanted to go in the room and help my mother. I wanted to wipe away her tears, place my head on her shoulders, and tell her that everything was going to be all right. I watched everything from behind the curtain and then moved away. Sometimes adults can seem so unapproachable.

The eight o'clock train is passing by while echoing its whistle as far as my bedroom. The train is coming from a different world; it travels from place to place every day, being a friend to many a lonely crowd in their time of need. Bringing people together. Setting people apart. Dada has not come home in a week. I wonder if he misses me.

I remember once I lost my most beautiful necklace. Dada bought me a better one. Dada has lost Ma, his most beautiful necklace. Did God find him a new one? I wish I had not received a new necklace. I wish I could find that old necklace. So Dada would not have to lose Ma. But obviously that is a child's dream.

Looking out from my bedroom window, I notice a girl playing with something. I ask her, 'Hey! What's that?' She shows me a necklace. It looks beautiful. Taking a closer look at it, I see that it looks a lot like the one I had lost. But this may just be my imagination. Sometimes things come back. Sometimes, despite all the differences, two people can be together because it comes down to the happiness of a very special person constituting one half of each of them. But a child's biggest achievement is to be a glue. It is to be better than Fevistick and Fevicol, someone who holds a family together.

Children have dreams other than receiving a letter from Hogwarts for their eleventh birthday. Little girls dream more than to be a princess. Children dream to make their parents feel special. They dream to make them happy. Today, I realise that I may have been unsuccessful at that.

Once Upon a Lifetime

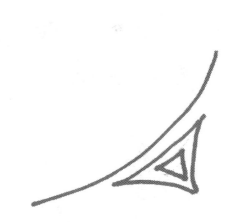

She could hear the conch shells blowing. She loved staring at the idol. The 'Ek Chala' goddess was decorated with ornaments made of silver foils known as *Daker Saaj*. The idol embodied the kindness of a mother with the fierceness of destroyer of all evil, all at once. Then she noticed him. He had his back to her. Then he turned. He smiled at her. She turned a little red. She was wearing a white Dhakai saree, his favourite. She had *shakha* (white bangles of conch shell) and *pola* (red bangles made of red coral) in both her hands. She had *loha*, a bangle made out of iron, and she wore red vermilion. She collected her sari about her and started walking towards him. The face of the goddess turned to that of her mother. She was furious. 'No, Mimi, never! I forbid you.'

'But, Ma, why?'

The goddess in her fury breaks the *shakha* and *pola* that Mimi was wearing. Mimi turned pale. 'Mother, what did you do? This is a bad omen. Don't you know, Ma?'

'Don't you know, Mimi? He is your brother!'

That was when she noticed Anindya's face turning pale, as he started walking away.

'Ani, wait Ani. Please,' she cried out as loudly as she could do, her lungs bursting out through her heart.

Mousumi woke up. She was to meet Anindya that day.

+ + + + + + + + + + + + + + +

Mousumi looked out of the window as she sipped hot tea. She was nervous. She was distracted. She spilt tea in her saucer, something she had not done in years. She could recollect her father saying, 'Mimi, don't be so absent-minded when you are drinking tea'. She could not drink her tea hot, even when she used to be young.

It now seemed like a forgotten song from a distant dream, something out of a fairy tale, something not real. She was meeting Anindya after a few decades. They got reconnected through some common relatives on Facebook, about six months back. She had often thought of sending him a friend request and then, at the last moment, prevented herself from doing so. Yet after he sent the friend request about six months back, they had chatted many a times. She had not dared to ask him about the last eighteen years; she had not dared to ask him why he never got in touch with her before. Last week, when he called her to say that he was coming to Calcutta and that he wanted to meet her, she could not believe it. How could she? The last time they spoke, it was eighteen years back; it was a stormy summer afternoon, and she could even now recall the howling of Nor'wester outside.

Once upon a time, Mousumi used to be 'Mimi' and Anindya was 'Ani', the only friend in Mimi's universe. Ani was now divorced, and she was a widow now. A lot of water had flown in the Ganges or in Thames at London, where he lived. In the eighteen monsoons that had passed since their last meeting, she had grown old, had wrinkles on her face, lost that glow in her eyes; and Ani's hairline had receded, and he had acquired a respectable paunch. Ani to her was just name engraved only in the tablet of her long-lost memories. They had led two separate lives in two very different continents for the last eighteen years. Now they would meet each other again and share a meal, just like they used to do at their ancestral home at Bag Bazar.

+ + + + + + + + + + + + + + +

'*Boudi*, shall I bring your tea?' It was Maina's mother. She used look after Mousumi, as a mark of gratitude since Mousumi took up the responsibility of Maina's education.

'Oh! What is the time now? Is it already four?'

'Yes, just about.'

Maina's mother looked out at the sky and muttered, 'Oh, look at the sky. Four in the evening in *Baisakh*, and it is so dark that it feels as though night has fallen. A Nor'wester is brewing, *Boudi*.'

Maina patted Sona, Mousumi's pet golden retriever. 'Sona, sweetie, the weather is really bad. You will miss your evening walk today,' said she as she stroked her gently.

She paused. 'I will get your tea. *Boudi*.' Then she looked at fully attired Mousumi and said, 'I think, you better cancel whatever errands you were planning to run.'

+ + + + + + + + + + + + + +

How could she not go? Mousumi remembered their Bag Bazar home. It was huge. There were so many families living under one roof that if one person yelled from one corner of the house, it would be hardly audible to someone else who lived in the other corner. Theirs was a joint family. It was a huge mansion built by her grandfather and his brothers, even before India's independence. You could get lost in the myriad rooms and balconies. It was a perfect location for them to play hide and seek during the monsoon season, when the streets would be waterlogged, and the water would not recede for days together. Mimi's parents, grandparents, and two other uncles lived there. So did her grandfather's other brothers and their extended family. It was a jamboree with a pandemonium going on at all times. Mimi was the youngest of the siblings. Only Anindya was close to her age. He was only four years senior to her. However, with everybody else much older than her, they formed a very strange alliance. They would fight about everything yet defend each other in all odd circumstances. Ani would always tell Mimi, 'You should be touching my feet. After all, I am your elder brother.'

And Mimi would retort, 'Oh my! I never realised you were so old.' She would add mischievously, 'Is that why your mother calls you *Buro*?'

Ani's nickname at home was 'Buro'. Ani would be furious and would chase Mimi around their huge portico.

During the Puja festivals when the younger people were supposed to touch the feet of their elders and seek blessings, Mimi would refuse to touch Ani's feet and would pretend to bless him instead.

As they grew older, they grew closer. With everybody else busy with their work, Ani and Mimi were thrown together. Ani would play the flute and Mimi would try to sing along with him. At the end of each music session, Ani would always pretend to thank Mimi and say, '*Thang Khau*', which though phonetically sounded like 'Thank you' meant 'eat your own leg' in Bengali. Mimi would be cross, and then Ani would beg for her forgiveness. After a while, they would be friends again.

There used to be fancy fares near Bag Bazar. Ani and Mimi used to go around with each other. At such a fare once, Mimi had loved the white and red bangles of *shakha* and *pola*. She wore them on her wrists till the shopkeeper noticed and snatched them away from her, telling them that the *shakha* and *pola* were meant for married ladies only. She had been deeply hurt, and knowing that she could not have them had somehow enhanced their value to her. The next day, Ani had smuggled for her a pair of *shakha* and *pola* from his mother's jewel box, where she kept spare ones for occasions only. Mimi had preserved them with care in her treasure chest.

+ + + + + + + + + + + + + +

Mousumi tucked in her hair. She put on a bindi. She had not put up one since her husband's demise—not that she missed him a lot. It was more because there was not enough reason to dress up any more. She wore an off-white sari with Dhakai designs. Ani used to be sold on traditional Dhakai sarees. He had told her that when she grows up, she would look lovely in them, yet he never cared to as much to come to her marriage, or at least let her know by a letter how beautiful she looked in the off-white Dhakai Jamdani at her reception. After all, he must have seen the snaps somewhere and realised that she had made the choice of an off-white Dhakai Jamdani just because of him, much to the chagrin of her mother, who was possibly the only one who could apprehend why she had chosen that dress. Her in-laws were very modern and broad-minded and appreciated their daughter-in-law's eye for fine things.

As she recollected, her eyes glowed with a new light, behind her thick rimmed glasses. As soon as she stepped outside, she heard the howling of the Nor'wester. Maina's mother was right. It was no day for a lady like her to venture out on the rough streets of Calcutta.

She hailed a taxi. She was finally going to meet Ani. She hardly cared that she was half drenched already.

+ + + + + + + + + + + + + +

Anindya was coming to the Coffee House for the first time in his life. For someone born and brought up in North Calcutta, that was a pretty strange thing. He had with great difficulty avoided coming here, because he had promised Mimi that they would be hanging out at Coffee House. He did not want be there without her. Today she was coming. He would be meeting her after eighteen long years; even Ram's* exile was less than that. He still remembered her in her multicoloured frocks with her legs dangling. He even remembered the first day she wore a sari.

He remembered cracks started forming in the team sometime when Mimi was around twelve years of age, when she realised what it meant to be a woman and that Ani was a man, not a woman. For some strange reason, he could never comprehend this change. He initially thought that Mimi was playing some kind of 'hard to get' game with him because he used to pull her leg too much. Eventually, he started missing her so much that he asked. He was heartbroken and confused when Mimi told him that now that she was grown-up, it would not be correct for her to go about their usual escapades.

Ani missed the afternoons when they would sneak out to Kumartuli and watch the craftsman carve out human forms out of mud, as they munched on peanuts that they bought for a paltry sum from Babu da, the local street vendor. They were sold on his peanuts. He used to love

---

*   —Ram of "Ramayan" was exiled for 14years

them and call them '*Manik-jor*'—twins that is—often giving them more than he should be.

He and Mimi would pick up every scrap of paper and junk plastic that they could collect from their household. They would sell it to the *kabariwallah* or junk man in the neighbourhood. They would save money till it was enough to buy candyfloss. She could even now hear the bell of the candyfloss seller calling out to all children, much like the Pied Piper of Hamelin. They would run and flock around the candyfloss man—Aamin was his name. They used to literally feast on the pink sticky candyfloss, which was called '*burimar chul*' (grandmother's hair).

Ani stared at the empty coffee cups in front of him He was early. He was early by almost two hours. 'Will she come?' he wondered. He had bought a copy of *Selected Poetry* by Goethe from Penguin Publishers. How he had wanted to share Goethe's love poems with her.

His wife Jane had complained that there were more than the two of them in their marriage. 'What had she meant?' He had thought of asking her. She had never known about Mimi. But women are very instinctive and can sense things without actually knowing anything concrete. Was he that enamoured of Mimi that he neglected Jane? He did not know what to believe.

He had wanted to meet Mimi after the tragic death of her husband. But he could not make it as he had promised his mother that he would never again meet Mimi in his lifetime. It was only last summer when his mother was at London and she realised how miserable he was that she relented.

As for him, he still missed Mimi; he held it against the world that it did not give them the chance to be the happy family they could have been. Mimi was like that part of the puzzle that could complete his life. He had often wondered why his mother had made him promise that he would never see Mimi. He felt angry towards his mother for his guilty conscious, which never allowed him to be happy in any other relationship. He hated his mother for making him stay away from the only person he wanted to be with.

He could still remember the last time he kissed her. He thought of Tagore: 'Whenever I hear old chronicles of love, it's age old pain, It's ancient tale of being apart or together.'

Theirs was a tale of being apart. Only, he had never imagined that been away from Mimi would make her more dear to him, make every moment that he spent with her so invaluable. He had never imagined that this separation would mean much more than all the relationships he ever had with all the women, culminated together.

'Clad in the light of a pole-star, piercing the darkness of time.
You become an image of what is remembered forever.'

+ + + + + + + + + + + + + +

Raindrops and small pieces of ice cubes lashed against the taxi window. Mousumi had hoped that Ani would come for her marriage. But he did not. She could not even ask anybody. Only her mother told her, 'Mimi, he is stuck with his studies in London. He would not be able to make it.'
'Yes, naturally, he was busy,' she had thought, 'with some English girlfriend definitely.'

Mousumi had started her married life with a vengeance to make it successful. Somehow she wanted to exact a revenge on Ani by being a good wife. Mousumi wanted to show him that she could be happy without him. Kingshuk had a modern outlook and encouraged Mimi to dress well, to carry herself well, and, most importantly, to be able to be independent, earn on her own right. And yes, given a little bit more time, he could have become a really good friend, good enough for her to forget Ani. But destiny had other plans, and in about five years' time, she found herself a widow. They were in an accident. Her husband succumbed to his injuries, and Mousumi recovered to find herself all alone, once again. They did not have a child to keep her busy; Kingshuk had wanted time for themselves before committing to a baby. Mousumi had expected Anindya to come down after her tragic loss and console her, yet she did not want him to know that all her happiness had always been around Ani, that even someone as charismatic and charming as Kingshuk could not change that for her.

It was a strange plethora of emotions when she learnt that Ani could not make it primarily because he was going through a bitter divorce after hardly a year of marriage. Apparently, his wife had claimed that their relationship was doomed from the very start. She had said, 'It was never just the two of us.' She never alluded to who the others were, though.

+ + + + + + + + + + + + + +

It was Mimi who decided that it was better to meet Ani at the Coffee House, the one place where you could have privacy in the middle of a crowd. Also, they had always wanted to come to the Coffee House together. It was better late than never.

'Didimoni, Coffee House is here.'

'Oh!' Mimi could not believe they she had already reached. That she had crossed eighteen years in half an hour.

'Should I wait for you?' asked the cabbie, who was from her road and knew her as the music teacher— Didimoni. 'No, it is OK, I will be late.'

She got in. Her eyes searched for Anindya. Then she figured him, sitting alone at the corner table, as a flash of lightning illuminated the smoke-filled room.

Then, there she was. It was like time travel. A Nor'wester was brewing that day also. She and Ani were sitting side by side as they listened to the raging winds outside. Once the wind subsided, Ani had asked Mimi to sing a song. She had sung a Tagore song, '*Je rate more duar guli bhanglo jhore*' (that stormy night when all my inhibitions were shattered).

All of a sudden, Ani had asked her passionately, 'Once, Mimi, just once, can I see you, as you really are?'

First, she had not understood. 'That is all I ask of you,' he had pleaded.

Then as she looked into his eyes, she saw his eyes burning with desire. She was dumbfounded. It was not in her power to deny him, defy him. She had taken off her dress, as if in a trance.

'You are so beautiful,' he kept muttering as he watched her.

'Can I please kiss your hands once? Please?' said Ani as he held her hands in his palms.

She could barely nod. Then he kissed and went on kissing her hands, and she started crying silently. She cried because it was a sin to be in love with one's brother, because it felt like heaven, because it was the end of innocence. She wanted him to kiss, her yet her conscience told her to stop him.

They were so engrossed that they had not noticed when Anindya's mother had come in.

'Anindya,' she had said, 'I want you to leave this room right now.'

'No, *Kaki*.' She referred to her aunt, Anindya's mother. 'He has not done anything, *Kaki*,' she had said desperately as she gathered her clothes about her. 'Please do not punish him. Please,' she had pleaded. Ani had looked at her, a resigned, pensive look that she still remembered.

That was the last time she saw Anindya. Their mothers discussed the situation that night. She did not see Anindya for the next week, as they went off to their maternal grandfather's home for a week. When she came back, she heard that Anindya had been sent off to a boarding school for better studies.

She had procrastinated on this over months. She would dream that Ani was back again. She had even imagined that they lived together in a place far away from Kolkata. She had thought about that evening a lot. She had blamed herself for it, always. Also her mother's constant reminder that it was a woman's duty to protect her honour under all circumstances never allowed her any respite.

Anindya smiled at her. Though he had aged, his smile remained the same. Her times with Ani in their Bag Bazar home swiftly flashed before her eyes like a kaleidoscope as she walked across the floor to Anindya's table.

Ani was there. 'Here you are. You look so beautiful, Mimi.'

Mimi had planned to pick up a fight with Ani for not coming to her marriage, not coming after her husband's tragic demise, and mostly for not keeping in touch with her for so many years. She could not do anything. She somehow instinctively knew he never forgot; he had never for a moment stopped hoping for them. One look into his eyes was enough.

As she sat down, she could feel the silent stream of tears, involuntary tears. She had not meant to cry, but she could not stop them. She looked at Anindya through a veil of tears.

Ani understood. He held her hand, looked into her eyes, and told her, 'Mimi, would you believe me if I told you that I have not kissed anybody that passionately ever in my life? Would you believe it?'

She could barely nod her head. 'Mimi, please don't cry, Mimi. Love like ours happens once in a lifetime, Mimi, that too only if you are very lucky.'

She was inconsolable. 'Why didn't you call me, Ani? We could have shared a lifetime together. God, I missed you so much.'

'Mimi, we have to be satisfied with just being best friends in this lifetime, Mimi, but in the next, you will be mine. I will not let you go. Never . . .'

He quoted Goethe . . .

> I saw you, felt your soul's outpouring
> In the sweet kindness of your gaze,

My heart was yours and all adoring,
Each pulse for you, each breathe your praise.

Mousumi and Ani spent the evening discussing all sorts of stuff, the books they loved, the movies they had watched; they reminisced about the happy times they had spent together. They talked about Calcutta, how it had changed, and about London, the river by Oxford, about Mimi's golden retriever Sona, about Kumartali and Durga Puja. Mimi invited Ani to spend the night in her apartment.

Maina's mother was curious, but she did not enquire. Mousumi was thankful. They chatted late into the night. Mousumi woke up in the morning; she prepared tea for Ani. She went to his room and called him. He did not respond. That was when Mousumi discovered that his body was cold. He looked restful, finally at peace with himself. His eyes were closed, and his hands were placed across his chest, as if he was just resting, waiting for Mousumi to bring his morning cup of tea.

He had kept a neatly wrapped brown paper packet beside his watch. Mousumi unwrapped the packet. There was a pair of pure white *shakha* and coral red *pola* on the side table. It was a sunny morning. She wanted to complete Ani's quote from his favourite poet:

> The rapture of your kiss must end
> Already, how my heart is aching,
> Seeing what grief your eyes portend!
> Downcast eyes, tears welling in distress,
> You stood, I stood, you watched me go
> And yet, Oh God, what happiness
> In being loved, in loving so!

Au Revoir, Bro

Amit smiled at Sumit as he drove his father Sumanta's new sedan. Sumit was all tensed up. 'Don't worry, I will drive safely,' he said.

Sumit smiled back with a nervous chuckle. 'You better, bro.'

Suddenly there was a blinding light, in front, on his right. It was a truck madly rushing in towards their sedan, like a glaring monster. Amit pressed the brake as hard as he could; there was a screeching sound; he could almost visualise his father's wrath, his face contorted in rage. Sumit stared at his brother, horror-struck, and then he felt the impact as the car swayed wildly. It was as if they were in a toy car. Before he could reach out to his brother and turn the steering wheel, a numbing pain paralysed him. He could feel the warm blood slowly draining away, his life force slowly draining away; his brother's white cotton shirt turned red. He surrendered to himself as he was pulled into a dark, swirling labyrinth.

+ + + + + + + + + + + + + +

Sumanta Das was a strict and disciplinarian father. He did not believe in being lenient with his sons. Sumit and Amit dreaded their father and followed his orders to the tee. Amit had to literally coax and cajole his elder brother,

Sumit, to let him drive. Sumit had finally relented when Amit emotionally blackmailed him, saying that it would be a long time before he came back from his first foreign tour.

Amit thought about all the excitement in his family and amongst his friends regarding his impending New York trip. There were excited calls from relatives and innumerable Facebook posts from his friends on his upcoming New York trip. It was not unusual for people to travel to New York for work in their profession, but he had just completed his graduation and joined this firm barely a year ago. It was a too short a time, even by the software industry standards, to be taken notice of and be selected for an overseas assignment.

He owed Sohini big time. It was largely because of the research project on telecom 4G that he had done with Sohini, at Jadavpur University, as a part of their curriculum. He had considered proposing to Sohini, before travelling to New York. He had been planning this for years. She was his best friend, yet he found it difficult to tell her how much he loved her. He was afraid that maybe in his quest for her love, he will lose Sohini as a friend. He had been through a lot of pain in the past when Sohini had fallen for somebody else. Amit had to keep a straight face and console Sohini, all the while pretending that he had not been aware of her dalliances. He had seriously thought of proposing to her before travelling to New York. He had deliberated a lot on this and finally decided that it would be best to propose once he was back from his New York assignment. He did not believe in the lost art of love letters, and he had not wanted to propose to her over the phone. What were the odds that she would refuse him? After all, they had known each other for a long time and were what you call 'best friends forever'. He would have been sure, had he not been aware of her past infatuation with Sumit. Sumit was not a nerd, unlike him. He was more athletic. He was good at academics, never excellent. It was his achievements in sports and his association with the students' union at Jadavpur University which made him popular. He was a strong and silent person and could mesmerise women inadvertently. There was a certain charming nonchalance about him, a devil-may-care attitude which attracted women likes flies to a flame.

Amit had dropped a message on Facebook for Sohini. 'If she felt the same way about him, she will reply' he thought. If she did, he would go to Mumbai soon after he was back from the United States, maybe en route. He would like to spend a couple of days with her. He also needed to talk to Sumit, understand if he was OK with it. Sumit was a pillar of strength to him, but he could never understand his brother's nonchalant attitude towards women in general and Sohini in particular. Then there was the blinding light.

+ + + + + + + + + + + + + + +

Suman—@Amit ... so NY really? So fast ... Congratulations ... take care ... don't fall in love with a blonde ... Sohini madam would be furious.

Sohini—@Amit ... great stuff. Lot of us even volunteered for non-Calcutta posting to further our careers. Yet you are the first one to make it to dreamland ... kudos ... as always, you always know what it takes to win ... @Suman ... stop pulling my leg ... at this rate, I will get a muscle cramp!

Amit—@Sohini. Seriously, muscle cramp? Always at your service, madam ... I am just a phone call away.

Suman—@Amit bravo, bravo. PJ Sir would have been over the moon. Krishna, the legendary lover, bows down his head to the lotus feet of his beloved Shri Radha—'*Dehi padapallavam udaram*'. You did not even attend his classes!

Amit—@Suman, thanks . . . this is the first time I am regretting not following the Baishnav *padabalis* at PJ's class too keenly. J

Sohini—@Suman . . . see, this is precisely why a lady cannot get serious around you guys. @ Amit . . . enough of naughtiness . . . now get serious . . . You will be at Big Apple in two days' time. I still cannot believe it.

Kunal—@Suman . . . please give 'Madam Serious' Miss Sohini a break . . . @ Amit . . . don't give a heart break to Sohini with misadventures with American hotties . . . @Sohini . . . don't worry. Even if Amit hits it off with a blonde @NY . . . We are five of us . . . '*Pancha Pandavas*' . . . always at your service . . . always at the service of the beautiful princess Draupadi . . . @Amit . . . hip . . . hip hurray . . . 'to the moon'! as Professor Calculus would say.

Suman—@Kunal . . . to America! to the moon! . . . @Sohini would you take all the five of us in marriage like Draupadi and be devoted to your 'Arjun'—Amit all your life?

Amit—@Suman . . . don't forget, unlike me, you are now in the same city as @Sohini . . . aren't you afraid of her highness? She will kill you with her eyes. @Kunal . . . Thanks and please don't get started on how your father's biggest mistake has been not to apply for a green card.

Sohini—@Kunal . . . I still remember how you had asked for a fork and a spoon on Amit's birthday . . . and I still remember Masima's flabbergasted expression . . . like she has been hit by a bolt from the blue . . . . @Amit . . . please update your Facebook status as soon as you land in the 'promised land' . . . and don't be naughty . . . So long . . .

Sumit—@Sohini . . . The 'fork and spoon' anecdote that you recounted is nothing . . . Kunal had actually asked Kakoli Madam, our class teacher, if he should put up his citizenship as 'American' in the Secondary Exam enrolment form. That was hilarious!

Amit—@*Pancha* Pandavas and @Sohini . . . I will definitely let you guys know as soon as I land . . . Wish me a safe journey.

Amit thought of leaving a message for Sohini, a one-to-one message. What should he write? He typed 'Gonna miss you'. No, he thought it would be too cheeky. He hit the Backspace.

'Can I be your Arjun?' . . . It was a bit too dramatic, and Amit knew Sohini had a lot more sympathy and respect for Karna than Arjun. She thought Arjun manipulated others to get what was best for him. She could go on for hours on Karna vs Arjun. Arjun definitely was not her favourite choice.
Ultimately he wrote as under:

@Sohini—six months will pass in a jiffy . . . my sweetheart . . . I have a lot to tell you . . . if you allow me time. BTW, if you find this message inappropriate, we shall forget it like a bad dream. If not, please reply back . . . Whatever happens . . . I will always be there for you.

+ + + + + + + + + + + + + +

Sumit realised that he was sitting in what seemed like a hospital bed. His hands were still shaking violently. He had to be stitched up. He had suffered a serious concussion and had six stitches on his forehead. The truck had barged into car perpendicularly . . . 'Where was the truck? Why couldn't Amit see it coming? And where is he now? Amit is supposed travel to America at the weekend,' he thought. The light was hurting his eyes. He could barely keep his eyes open. He cried out, 'Where is Amit?' He was not sure if he was audible as the doctors and nurses did not seem to hear him. It seemed like a bad dream. Soon, the sedatives kicked in, and he was sucked into a soft, caring world of drowsiness and sleep.

When he regained consciousness, he slowly remembered. He had gone to pick up Amit from his office at Sector Five. Amit was excited to see him with the brand new Honda Civic and requested his permission to drive back home. Sumit was very firm.

He told Amit, 'Our father has told me very clearly, Amit.'

'Bro, I will be off to New York in the weekend. Please let me drive.'

'OK, but nobody can know. OK?'

'Yep!'

'And please be careful. If you damage his new car, Father is going to de-skin me, literally.'

'Yes, Big Bro. I will be careful.'

The doctor came and told him that he would be released next day. When he enquired about Amit, the doctor hesitated a little and then said, 'I am sorry.' It took some time for it to sink in. Still he could not believe it. He had survived just fine. Why would it be any different for Amit? Amit's smile still flashed before his eyes.

'My dad? My mom?' he blurted out.

'Your parents have gone to the crematorium for the last rites of your brother,' the doctor added.

He could not believe that his brilliant little brother, who was so close to living his American dream, was no more. He could not believe his dorky little brother, whom he protected against bullies at school, bullies on their street, was no more. And he, Sumit, had survived. He could not but blame himself for Amit's untimely demise. When he had handed the keys to Amit, little did he know that if it would their last ride together. Why did he let Amit drive? He was the elder brother. It was his duty to protect Amit.

The next morning when Sumit woke up, he was convinced that it was really a bad nightmare. It was only when Sumanta came in, his eyes swollen, did he realise that his worst fears had been realised. He literally had murdered Amit. He could not accept that he was the one responsible for the untimely demise of his brother.

Amit was never much into sports. He was the studious type; with his thick glasses and pale demeanour, he was very unlike Sumit. His lack of sporting qualities were more than compensated for by his genius and his sweet disposition. Only, when he smiled widely, his protruding canines added a mischievous dimension to his character.

Sumit felt as if he had been hit hard near his ribs; the world reeled under his feet, and darkness engulfed him from all sides, choking him. He could hardly breathe. Sumanta rushed to his side and held him tightly. 'Let us go home, Son,' he said as he hugged Sumit. Sumit was dumbfounded. He surrendered himself in the strong arms of his father, something he had not done for a very long time.

+ + + + + + + + + + + + + + +

Sohini blushed as she read Amit's Facebook message. She regretted not logging into Facebook for one whole day.

She replied, 'My sweetheart . . . I shall always talk about this message . . . but only with you . . . I had thought I could put my feelings aside once I was out of Kolkata . . . put a distance between us . . . I forgot . . . distance can also make the heart grow fonder . . . miss you already . . . Reply to me as soon as you reach NY . . .'

Sohini had almost given up hope. She had even assumed the worst. She was afraid that Amit will never propose. Sohini had what you call a teenage crush or infatuation on Sumit. He was the president of the college union and the college sports star too. Every girl in the campus wanted to be his girlfriend. Sohini wanted too. She was beautiful, and she was accomplished. She only made the mistake of supposing that Sumit also was in love with her. The one person she found solace in, when her dreams crumbled, was her childhood friend Amit.

+ + + + + + + + + + + + + + +

He was home, when he woke up the next morning. He watched his mother, Surupa, as she meticulously arranged an ironed full shirt of Amit and spread it on the bed, in such a way that it seemed that somebody was wearing it. Amit, being the weaker sibling, had been his mother's favourite. He had expected her to be inconsolable. But she did not betray any signs of grief, only a silent residual sadness, worse than grief. He watched her as she folded the cuffs neatly, spread the trouser to full length, with the shirt dangling over the trouser, rather than tucking it in, just like Amit used to do. She then folded Amit's handkerchief with his name embroidered on it, a reminiscence of Surupa's embroidery skills, and placed it beside the full shirt, along with his oddly shaped Timex watch. Amit always wore a full shirt, across the year. He found half shirts and T-shirts uncomfortable, a direct contrast to Sumit, who always felt more comfortable in his tees. He was mesmerised as he watched Surupa spray Amit's favourite AXE deodorant on the underarms of the shirt. She then sprayed Polo, a Calvin Klein perfume that Surupa had gifted Amit after he got his job last year. Amit was a connoisseur of perfumes, and he wore the Polo sparingly on special occasions only. Sumit watched Surupa as she went about her ritual in silence. Surupa then opened the aluminium frame window looking out to the lake and stared out, like Amit would. Her trance was broken by the sound of calling bell. Neighbours, relatives, and acquaintances were pouring in. Sumit quietly slipped into the room, after Surupa left to attend the neighbours who had come to offer their condolences. It seemed as if he were stealing into a scared place where he did not belong. He lay down just beside the shirt and trouser arrangement on the other side of the bed, just beside his brother's shirt and trouser. He placed his hand across the shirt, as if he was holding his little brother, just the way they used to sleep in their younger days. Sumit and Amit had been like Siamese twins during their childhood days. As he closed his eyes and inhaled the perfume, he could almost feel Amit.

He looked around Amit's room, exploring it in a way he had never done before. They had grown apart over the last couple of years due to possibly varied interests that they pursued. His eyes scanned Amit's bookshelf. What was he looking for? There was a photo frame—a photo of Amit and his friends. '*Pancha* Pandavas and Darupadi' was scrolled in black permanent marker below the photo. He recognised only Sohini. Right beside it was a broken eyeglass frame. It was oddly familiar. The glass was shattered, and the entire thing was carefully assembled together with Sellotape and black tape and possibly generous amount of adhesive. There it was on Amit's corner shelf, displayed like a trophy, like a decorative display piece.

Sumit remembered that there was this bully Sambhu, who had taken to harassing Amit. Sambhu had started calling him '*Pagla* Dasu' or 'Mad Dasu'. They had ganged up on Amit on Holi and drenched him with colour and tar. In the commotion that ensued, Amit lost his eyeglasses, which were trampled on. They threatened him of dire consequences, if any of it reached his or their parents. When Amit returned home, he was traumatised. He would not tell anybody who had done it to him. When Sumit pestered him, he told Sumit in confidence about his humiliation.

'They ridiculed me. They distorted my name and called me "*Pagla* Dasu".'

Sumit could not suppress his smile. 'OK, they have taken the pains of reading Sukumar Ray and have even intelligently named you, Amit Das, as "Mad Dasu". You must admire their sense of humour.'

'Bro, they insulted me. After today, I will be a laughing stock,' said Amit.

Sumit turned serious and said, 'Sorry, Bro. Don't you worry.' He did not utter a word to anybody. On the day after Holi, Sambhu personally apologised to Amit, in the field, in front of everybody and handed him the poorly reassembled eye gear, as a memento. Sambhu even added, 'You know, you should have really told me that you are the little brother of Sumit.' Amit enjoyed the turn of events, though he and Sumit did not discuss it ever. Amit had preserved the mended spectacles. Sumit realised for the first time what it had meant to his brother.

He quietly went up to their attic. He looked into the wardrobe for boxes where Surupa had meticulously stored stuff from their childhood and adolescence. He found old comic books of *The Phantom* and *Mandrake the Magician*. Comic books that they used to treasure much before Clarke Kent, Peter Parker, and Bruce Wayne took over the mantle of 'Super Hero'. He found a stamp album, something that Amit had collected over the years, and a box full of plastic animal figures that used to come free with Binaca toothpaste. He remembered how Amit used to collect the figures and store them in little tin box.

The entire week their home was thronged with visitors. Everybody tried to console them; everybody sympathised with them for their loss. Sumit had expected people to accuse him, criticise him, and raise a finger at him for his callousness. But nobody blamed Sumit; instead, everybody sympathised with them. It was uncomfortable and unbearable. He wanted to scream out loudly and confess that it was his fault that his brother was no more. He had failed his brother. Only Nakakima (his parental aunt), blinded by her grief, demanded to know how come Amit was driving the car when Sumit was right there. Sumanta again came to his rescue. 'Na'di,' he said, 'I had asked Sumit to give the keys.'

'You know, he would have been required to drive in the States.' Sumanta added. 'Also, he was never an irresponsible driver. The truck driver was drunk. He was tired after driving the truck continuously for over twelve hours. It is really his fate, Na'di. Let us pray for the soul of Amit,' Sumanta concluded.

Nobody talked about it after Sumanta reprimanded Nakakima in no uncertain terms.

Sumit wanted to demand from his father why he was lying blatantly and defending him, even though Sumit had gone against his father's advice and handed the car keys to his brother. He wanted to scream, 'It was I who gave him the keys, Baba. Not you.'

Sumit again went into Amit's room that evening. He noticed that the computer was still on and so was the broadband. 'Let them be on,' he thought. He sat down on his brother's chair and looked at the photo frame. Amit looked so happy with Sohini. Sohini, possibly, was another reason why they had drifted apart.

He remembered Sohini well enough. It was four years or so back. She had come to meet Amit, and nobody was home.

'Is Amit home?'

'No, he is not. But he should be back soon. Would you like to wait?'

'That would be good.'

Sumit had taken her to his room. 'My room is in a mess. But please sit.'

She sat on the corner of his bed, her hands folded on her knees.

He had heard a rumour that Sohini had a crush on him. 'Sohini, is it OK, if I light a cigarette?' he asked her as he noticed the miniscule beauty spot, just below the right corner of her lips. As she smiled, it extended to her spot. She seemed nervous. It was awkward.

'Would you like to listen to music while you wait?'

'It would be good,' said Sohini, barely lifting her eyes. Her voice quivered like a leaf in a storm.

He put on one of his favourites of Clapton—'Wonderful Tonight'.

> We go to a party, and everyone turns to see
> This beautiful lady that's walking around with me.

And then she asks me, 'Do you feel all right?'
And I say, 'Yes, I feel wonderful tonight.'

Sumit casually remarked while he smoked his cigarette, 'There is a rumour about you and me going around in the campus. I hope you don't mind it.'

He turned to her and smiled. 'It feels good to know I am coveted by a beautiful lady, like you, even if it is only a rumour,' he said.

Sohini was very silent. Sumit thought he might have offended her and quickly added, 'I know there is no basis to it really.'

'Really?' whispered Sohini.

Was she crying? Sumit threw his cigarette and came quickly to Sohini's side. She really was crying.

'Are you OK?' he asked.

She looked up. 'What if, all of it is true?'

It was then that he had kissed her, without planning it and maybe without even meaning it. Sumit was too busy with sports and enjoying his stint as the college student union president to be serious about a lady. Every girl on the campus wanted to be the 'First Lady' of the campus, and Sumit enjoyed that attention too much to fall for one woman. He had not meant to kiss her; it was an intoxicated moment on a summer afternoon. It was almost surreal. She was not Sohini, and he was not Sumit. They were as if caught in another space and time. Sumit was not the flirting type. He had reflected a lot on why he had kissed Sohini that day. Even he had not been able to understand. He had often wondered how it would have been to share life with Sohini. But somehow, he knew it was not to be. It was not in his destiny to be with her. Sohini was always destined to be with Amit. He had seen them laugh together. He knew. He was surprised that they did not know. Whenever he used to think about what had happened that afternoon, he thought of Ghalib: '*Yeh na thi hamari kisamat ki vishal e yaar hota'* (It was not our destiny that we meet as beloved).

Sohini had been hurt beyond words when she realised that Sumit had not meant that afternoon to happen. It was a rejection she had found too hard to handle and had even contemplated to end her life. It was Amit who had found her, comforted her, given her hope. She found solace with her friend Amit, though somehow it seemed to her that theirs was beyond the conventional realms of friendship.

As for Sumit, he might have pretended to the world that he had been righteous, but deep inside, he knew that though he did not have an affair with Sohini, he had done worse. Sumit let everyone on the campus realise that Sohini had a crush on him, and then he, being the cool guy, feigned ignorance. When he found Sohini and Amit had drawn closer, he felt happy but not without a tinge of regret.

He reminisced and thought, 'I had been the epitome of evil.' He had been selfish. He had led Sohini on, knowing well that Amit had a soft corner for her—all this, even though he was not even remotely interested in her.

+ + + + + + + + + + + + + + +

On the tenth day when Amit's religious rites were to be done, Sumanta insisted that Sumit conduct the same on behalf of the family. Sumit was utterly confused. Didn't he just kill his only brother? He was fully aware how Amit had been traumatised by Sohini falling for his 'cool big brother'. Yet he had taken advantage of Sohini.

He did not want to be the one to conduct the *Sradh*. But his father convinced him.

The priest chanted from Bhaghvat Gita, after the religious rituals were over. Sumit listened with rapt attention.

> *na jayate mriyate va kadacin*
> *nayam bhutva bhavita va na bhuyah*
> *ajo nityah sasvato 'yam purano*
> *na hanyate hanyamane sarire*

(The soul is never born nor dies at any time. Soul has not come into being, does not come into being, and will not come into being. Soul is unborn, eternal, ever-existing, and primeval. Soul is not slain when the body is slain.)

Sumit understood why his father had insisted on him performing the rituals.

> *vasamsi jirnani yatha vihaya*
> *navani grhnati naro 'parani*
> *tatha sarirani vihaya jirnany*
> *anyani samyati navani dehi*

(As a human being puts on new garments, giving up old ones, the soul similarly accepts new material bodies, giving up the old and useless ones.)

He cried, for the first time in ten days. He went on crying and could not stop himself. The priest asked his father if he should stop the services. His father just said, 'Let him cry.' Sumanta then sat with his son, and they mourned for Amit together. Sumanta held Sumit's hand tightly as the priest continued the Bhagwat Gita narration.

> For certain is death for the born,
> and certain is birth for the dead;
> therefore, over the inevitable you
> shouldn't grieve.

+ + + + + + + + + + + + + + +

Kunal—@Amit . . . what happened? No news . . . Did you forget your friends as soon as you landed in America?

Suman—@Kunal don't be jealous . . . he has just landed . . . give the man some time.

Kabir—guys, guys . . . cool idea . . . let's find out from Masima . . . I can go down if you want . . . (I am the only one at Cal . . . Hurray!) . . . Masima makes the most amazing potato chips.

Suman—@gastronomic Kabir . . . give it a break . . . @ Sohini madam, did you hear from Amit?

Sohini—Not yet, *yaar*.

Sohini was hurt that Amit had not written back to her. It was nearly a week.

Kunal—Relax, man. Give him some time to settle down . . .

Subroto—Hey guys, uploaded some snaps of our farewell . . . Hey @Sohini . . . looks like Amit only had eyes for you . . . check out the pics and videos . . .

Sohini browsed through the pics. They were lovely. Specially the video of Amit singing '*Tomake Cai*' (I want you) of Suman Chattopadhyay . . . slightly out of tune but lovely.

+ + + + + + + + + + + + + + +

It was that night that Sumit went to his brother's room again. The computer was still on. He logged in. The Internet Explorer was still open; Amit's Facebook password was automatically saved. He opened Amit's Facebook account. It was flooded with updates from all his friends.

He started reading all the postings on his brother's Facebook page. He read Sohini's message. That was when tears again clouded his vision. He wrote on Amit's wall:

> Amit loved you all . . . but God loved him more than anyone of us . . . he has left for his heavenly abode on the 9th of this month. Signing off for the last time on behalf of Amit . . . Au revoir . . . till you meet again in this world or any other, in this lifetime or maybe another.

> As Richard Bach has said, 'A farewell is necessary before you can meet again and meeting again, after moments or lifetimes, is certain for those who are friends.'

> He is gone yet he is with each one of us, who loved him and who he loved . . . and so long as we remember him and love him . . . he will be there with us.

My Beloved Doesn't Speak
To Me Any More

It was well beyond midnight. Sucharita was at her canvas. She worked best during the night. Playing with colours was her dream, her passion. She was trying to recreate the train scene from *Pather Panchali*. Apu and Durga running across fields of *kash* flowers to get a glimpse of the steam engine train. The smoke of the train against the blue sky and fluffy white cloud was an exquisite image. Suddenly the canvas was animated, and there was her father running with Apu on his back. 'Baba, come back,' she wanted to shout, yet her voice betrayed her. Her father smiled back at her. Then there was a loud explosion, and he was gone. She looked with horror as a streak of blood red slowly engulfed her canvas.

Sucharita almost fell from her chair, managing her canvas on the easel at the last moment. She could never get over losing her father in the Bangladesh War. She would sometimes have these hallucinations about her father, when she sat at her aisle for a night out.

+ + + + + + + + + + + + + +

Yousuf had reached the wedding party early, and Barun and Ishita were late, as always. Yet it was Ishitas's cousin's marriage. But then they were coming all the way from their offices at Salt Lake, Sector V, unlike him. Unlike the software firms, all major advertising firms had their offices in and around Park Street. He was a junior creative consultant. All he knew was that Ishita's cousin, Ruchita, was getting married. He could not locate any other acquaintance in the gathering.

It was then that he noticed this beautiful lady, a garland of jasmine worn around her hair. Yousuf had always liked the traditional Bengali attire. It always reminded him of the Pujas when he went out with his friends on pandal-hopping. Even Ishita, who normally always preferred jeans and T-shirt, would get dressed in a sari during Pujas. It made her look beautiful. There was a certain something about a sari. It magically transformed a mere girl into a woman.

Yousuf noticed that the lady had a bindi on, her head was covered with a streak of vermilion, and she was wearing the traditional Bengali wedding bracelets called *shakha* and *pola*—one red and the other white. As he stared at her, she suddenly looked at him and smiled, as if they had known each other for ages. It was as if she knew him from a half-remembered past.

Then she called out, 'Can you hear me?'
'Yes,' he said as if in a trance; subconsciously, he thought it was odd the way she had called him. It was actually a traditional way of Bengali women calling their husbands as it was considered impolite to call your husband by his name in public.
'Why don't you come here and help me with the decorations?' she called.
The lady was painting art motifs with rice paste to mark the auspicious occasion of the wedding. Yousuf loved *alpona* and had a special knack for it. He merrily joined in. It was better than waiting like an idiot for Barun and Ishita to show up. His frustration melted away as he

helped the lady in painting the patterns and motifs of *alpona* with rice paste.

It was a while before he realised that they were a cynosure to others in the wedding. He was surprised. He had not consciously done anything inappropriate, though he was enjoying the lady's company. It was obvious that she was an accomplished artist in her own rights. He complimented her, and she laughed. She told him, 'Well, painting has always been my way of expression, but I never realised you were so much into painting too.'

It seemed as if people were staring at them and discussing them in whispered tones. Was it because the lady was married? That is when he noticed that Barun and Ishita had finally turned up. He excused himself. 'My friends are here.'

'Be back soon,' she said.

He smiled broadly at his friends, and he stared at them; he realised that Ishita's face was pale, devoid of colour, and his smile faded.

'What happened?' he asked.
'You have to leave now!' she urged.
'Why?'
'Let's please get into your car, Barun. Can we, please?'
Ishita asked Barun to drive towards Outram Ghat. She did not say a word till the time they reached.
They went to the Outram Ghat waterfront hangout, Scoop—the ice cream parlour.
Finally, Ishita demanded, 'How did you happen to speak to her?'
'You mean the lady?'
'Yes, Yousuf, yes!'

'She called me, Ishita. Who is she, anyway? Why were people staring at us? Why did you bring us here?'

'That is my cousin Sucharita.'

Then she whispered to herself, 'I should have realised that you resemble him too much.'

Yousuf could not hold himself back. 'Whom do I resemble?'

'You resemble, Amir. He is the man that my sister thinks she is married to.'

'But she is married. She was wearing vermilion.'

She looked at Yousuf strangely. 'Do Muslim married women wear vermilion, Yousuf?'

'I am confused. She was wearing conch shell wedding bracelets too!'

'Yes, Yousuf. That is the tragedy. She thinks she is married to Amir. She is normal in every other way.'

+ + + + + + + + + + + + + + +

Sucharita had come to invite Ronnie for her birthday party. *Ustadji's* classical music class was the easiest place to get him, as he was the quintessential restless, rebellious young man as such. He only never missed *Ustadji's* lessons. Sucharita was also picking up classical music in pursuit of her dream project of integrating the art forms of painting and music.

As everybody waited for *Ustadji*, Amir sang to entertain all. He sang,

> *Saawan Beeto Jaye Pe Harwa*
> *Saawan Beeto Jaye Pe Harwa*
> *Mann Mera Ghabraye*
> *Mann Mera Ghabraye*

(Monsoon passes by my loved, my heart is anxious for you).

Ustadji was a versatile classical maestro; music was his life. He used to tell his disciples that musical creativity required a bit of tragedy, an understanding of the pain of love, love and loss. Many students came to *Ustadji* to learn music; sarod players, *surbahar* players, and sitar players flocked to *Ustadji's* place to learn the essence of classical music.

Amir looked up and saw Sucharita. 'I am looking for Ronnie', she whispered. Amir indicated with his eyes where Ronnie was, but his concentration was broken. That was the first day that Amir missed *taal* or beat. For the first time in his life, Amir's beloved was not his music. All his years of dedication and sacrifice, all his melody, they seem to have been only waiting for Sucharita.

Ronnie was good at sitar, but it was more of entertainment for him than a means of livelihood. His knowledge of classical music gave him a certain edge over other less-privileged men. Ronnie was a ladies' man. And he really knew how to play it to the gallery. He had learnt classical music on the insistence of his grandfather, who was a classical exponent and a close acquaintance of *Ustadji*. Though he was not serious about classical music, being with *Ustadji* gave him an inner peace that had eluded him otherwise. Ronnie was a pragmatic person.

'What were you telling, Amir?'
'What? Nothing really. I was looking for you actually.'
'Sucharita, we have never seen Amir speak to a lady, ever.'
'You must be joking, Ronnie.'
'No, I am damn serious. But do not mess with him. He is *Ustadji's* favourite.'
'Then he must be someone special.'
'That he is. Ustadji is grooming Amir personally. He has very high hopes on him.'

He added, 'If you hear Amir, you would know what he means.'

'You sound as if you are either jealous of Amir or in awe of him.'

Ronnie smiled, 'Tell me, madam, what made you cross your temple and come to mine?' He pulled her leg.

Sucharita was a painter. She had been a disciple of Bikash Bhattacharya. She and Ronnie would argue all the time on which was a better creative medium. Was it painting, or was it singing? Was the visual medium superior, or was audio medium superior?

'Don't pull another fight now,' said Sucharita in mock anger. 'I came to invite you for my birthday party.'

'Seriously, only over-pampered rich kids celebrate their twenty-fifth birthday.'

'Well, I might not be that rich, but yes, I am a little pampered.'

'Little! Your practically lord over your uncle, Suchi.'

'It happens, Ronnie. If you lose your father to a stupid war . . .' She was suddenly serious.

She pushed back her tears and smiled, 'Be there on Friday.'

'OK, madam, I will be there.'

Sucharita had lost her mother at birth, and she lost her father in the Bangladesh War. Her father, an army officer, had been rescuing a group of endangered refugees when he was caught unawares by a group of estranged Pakistani soldiers. Sucharita's maternal uncle had raised Sucharita and his own daughter Ruchita equally. He had pampered and spoilt them in every way possible. Sucharita and Ruchita's birthdays were days he insisted on celebrating.

As she passed, Sucharita stopped to hear Amir singing 'Mora saiyaan mose bolena' (my beloved doesn't speak to me any more). As she listened, she was moved to tears. She thought, 'That is a voice that can move heaven and earth.'

Amir had avoided all human contacts throughout his life, always afraid of distraction. He had built imaginary walls around him, protecting himself like a porcupine. The only person he was close to was his mother. Amir's father passed away when he was at a tender age. Amir's mother had spent all her life in pursuit of Amir's music career. Her father was a great exponent of Indian classical music, and that was how she got acquainted with *Ustadji*. Amir's mother was his rock of Gibraltar. He knew that falling for Sucharita would be wrong in every way. It would doom his career, destroy all the dreams he had built for so many years. He sang away,

> *Saawan Beeto Jaye Pe Harwa*
> *Saawan Beeto Jaye Pe Harwa*
> *Mann Mera Ghabraye*
> *Mann Mera Ghabraye.*

And she did not even speak to him. He smiled at himself *"Mora saiyaan mo se bole na"*—My beloved doesn't speak to me.

For the first time in so many years, Amir went back home and had very little 'musical news' to share with his mother. When his mother asked about his day, he had hardly anything to tell her. His day had been around Sucharita, and he was not in a position to tell his widowed mother that he had wasted the entire day thinking of this lady.

The next day itself, Amir actually asked Ronnie who Sucharita was. 'Is she your fiancée or friend?' he asked Ronnie awkwardly.

'Well, we know each other practically from our childhood days. We grew up on the same street, had the same fights. Technically, she is a friend. But why are you asking?'

Amir blushed. 'I just wanted to know more about her.'

Ronnie was amused. 'Well, she is an artist, has a couple of exhibitions to her credit too. She believes you can paint a song, you can paint a raga.'

Amir was excited. 'Has she ever done any?'

'Yes, mostly made some feeble attempts at it. But you should have seen her painting on Bhairav, a curious mix of a painting of dawn with inspired colours floating across the canvas like a mad streak. That is what she thinks to be her masterpiece, so far. Hence her interest in classical music.'

'Wow! That is so amazing!'

'Would you like to get introduced to her?' asked Ronnie.

Amir blushed again. 'No, not like that. Just that someone can think so beautifully of fusing painting and music. It is amazing. She is one amazing woman.'

'That she is.'

'I have never met anybody with such a beautiful mind.'

Ronnie understood that Amir was falling for Sucharita. He quipped, 'She has a beautiful mind and a body to match. Several men have drowned themselves in the mystic mind of Sucharita. Don't let her be your waterloo, Amir. You have to focus on your music.' Amir was in too much of a dream world to realise what he meant.

'If only you could have introduced me to her.'

Ronnie was surprised and exasperated. He finally said, 'It is her birthday this Friday. I can get you invited.'

'Can you please?' said Amir eagerly.

Amir went home that day on cloud nine. He was invited to Sucharita's birthday. That evening, he confided in his mother. He asked her, 'Ma, do you think it is possible to paint a Hindustani classical raga with colours?'

'Some would say that both the forms are similar in more than one ways.'

'How, Ma?'

'Well, you have seven *swaras* of a *sargam,* and you have seven colours of rainbow. Maybe you can match the seven notes to seven colours, one colour for each musical note.'

'Ma, how do you think this way, Ma? You know, Ma, there is this lady, Sucharita. She is really a painter, and she thinks that she can paint ragas.'

'Amir, I have never seen you so moved by anybody.'

'Ma, by the same logic, I should able to sing a song on Van Gogh's *Sunflowers* or maybe *The Potato Eaters.*'

Meher Begum understood that her son was, for the first time in his life, in love. Amir did not sleep the entire night. In the morning, he was all exuberant. 'Ma, I think I know how you can sing a song on *Sunflower*s. Ma, would you please listen to my recital?'

'Amir *jaan*, you should be doing your *riwaz, jaan*. You should not waste your time on famous paintings, *jaan*.'

'No, Ma, you must listen. Please, Ma.'

'You know, I think I can even compose notes for *The Red Vineyard, The Yellow House* or *The Night café.*'

Meher Begum listened to her son's amazing fusion of classical music and Vincent Van Gogh. She knew for sure that he was in love.

Sucharita has been admired by many men. She was used to getting compliments. She despised men who fell for her desperately. She found them shallow and cheap. Ronnie was the only friend who was a man and whom she had stuck to since her childhood days. She herself found it strange that she got along so well with Ronnie, a self-professed playboy.

+ + + + + + + + + + + + + + +

'I saw Amir make a complete fool of himself.'

Ronnie was not surprised. 'Well, he is a genius as far as music is concerned. Take him out of music, and he is like fish out of water.'

'No, I don't want to insult your best friend.' Sucharita smiled and added, 'But in everything else, he behaves absolutely like a nitwit. Had I not heard him sing, I wouldn't have believed someone like him can sing so well.'

'Geniuses are like that, Sucharita. He is not Ronnie.'

'No, he is not Ronnie. And luckily so, as Ronnie is my best friend,' said Sucharita with a wide smile on her face.

That evening, Amir sang his latest composition 'The Sunflower' for the guests at Sucharita's party. 'When I first met Sucharita, someone told me that she could paint Hindustani classical ragas, and I was amazed. It is she who inspired me to attempt a music composition on Vincent Van Gogh's *Sunflowers*.'

Sucharita was not the only one to be amazed. Everybody could only talk about Amir's rendition.

'Do you sing at birthday parties?' Sucharita's uncle was interested.

'No,' he blurted out. 'All this was for Sucharita only.'

He did not notice Sucharita's smitten smile turn contemptuous. Ronnie noticed. He mentally decided to discuss with Amir and make him understand why it would be best to forget Sucharita. Sucharita never got over her father's death. She always blamed the war in particular and Muslims in general for tearing her family apart. She might come to love the art of Amir, but she would never be able to accept him as her friend. To her mind, it would be a betrayal to her father's memory. Ronnie had to explain to Amir.

Amir did not give Ronnie any chance. He proposed to Sucharita that night itself, when the birthday party was almost over.

'Sucharita, there are seven notes in music and seven colours in a rainbow.'

Sucharita listened on, silently.

'Sucharita, I have never loved anyone, and I would never love anybody else so much. Can you please allow me to fuse my music and your painting to create a beautiful world for ourselves?' He was over the moon. He was somehow confident that she would not refuse him. He had seen admiration in her eyes when he was singing.

Sucharita could not help herself; the contemptuous smile spreading over her beautiful bright face made her look dangerous.

'Have you any idea how I hate your people? You, you are the reason that I lost my father,' she said in a barely audible voice. 'Who do you think you are, Amir? Do you even know me? I lost my father to your people.'

Amir was shell-shocked.

Sucharita continued, 'Yes, that is the truth. What do you think, Amir? Just because you have a mellifluous voice, Amir, do you think you can get away with anything?'

She continued as if that insult was not enough. 'Have you ever heard yourself when you speak? You sound stupid, Amir. You are so naive.'

Amir was practically in tears. He had never been so insulted in his life. He stumbled out of Sucharita's home.

He had not noticed the car rushing at him from nowhere. Ronnie immediately took him to the hospital. Sucharita was stunned. She could not believe that she had been so cruel that she had practically pushed Amir in front of a running car. How was she any different from the heartless people who had taken her father away?

Amir passed away late in the night. Ronnie was there at the hospital, throughout the night. In the morning, when he went to meet Sucharita, she was in tears. She wanted to see Amir, for one last time.

Ronnie took her to Amir's home. Meher Begum was bidding her son farewell in the best way that she knew, by singing a raga. Her eyes were swollen from crying all night. By the morning, she had composed herself and wanted to give a proper send-off to her beloved son. The instant she met Sucharita, she knew that she was the lady that her son had talked about. She was not aware that Sucharita's insults had driven Amir to his accident. She held Sucharita's hand and told her '*Jaan*, you really are beautiful. Amir has told me a lot of things about you? Would you show me your painting of Bhairav, some day?'

Sucharita was stunned. She did not know how to answer Meher Begum's polite questions. Meher Begum held her hand.

'You know, *jaan*, you two would have made a very beautiful couple. But you know, "*Waqt se aage aur kismet se zyada, kuch nehi milta*"' (you can never get anything before your time and more than your destiny).

Sucharita cried silently in Meher Begum's arms. She cried for her father; she cried for Amir. Amir was buried that day itself. Sucharita did not attend the burial. Ronnie made sure that she returned home.

Next day, when he went to meet Sucharita, he was shocked. She was wearing vermilion on her head and wore red and white bangles on her hands, like a married woman. She gladly told him, 'You have to visit me more often. After all, I am now Sucharita Ali, wife of your best friend, Amir Ali.'

She was raving mad. How would she know that wearing vermilion was a strict Hindu ritual? To her, it did not matter. She was OK in all other respects; only, she called herself Sucharita Ali and dressed like a married lady.

Ronnie was stunned. Sucharita sensed his reluctance and told him, 'Why don't you wait for a while? He will be home soon. You know, I should not take his name. Next, I am planning to paint Khamwaz—"*Mora saiyaan mose bolena*". Do you know it, Ronnie? My Amir sings it to perfection. Now I shall paint it.'

Ronnie was at a complete loss for words. He blamed himself for bringing the two people he loved most together. He had never in his worst nightmares imagined losing them both. One was driven to death by love, and the other was driven to madness by death. Ronnie would never love in his life again.

Ishita ended her narrative. It was almost morning. The ice cream parlour had closed long back, and the three friends had effectively spent the night on the banks of Ganges at Outram Ghat. The morning sun was reluctantly saying goodbye to the moon that still lingered over the horizon.

Ishita turned to Yousuf. 'The first day I met you, Yousuf, on our orientation day, you asked me why I had been staring at you. You resemble Amir to a great extent, Yousuf, that's why. I should have known better than to invite you to Ruchita's wedding. It's entirely my fault,' she added.

'No, it's not Ishita,' said Yousuf, realising for the first time why she had avoided his advances so long. 'Just because I resemble somebody, it is not necessary that our story should also be this tragic. Believe me, Ishita.'

He stood there as Ishita cried silently in his arms. He held her tight. It was morning. It was another day, another beautiful day, and all he wanted was to do was to hold his '*saiyaan*' in his arms.

The Redemption

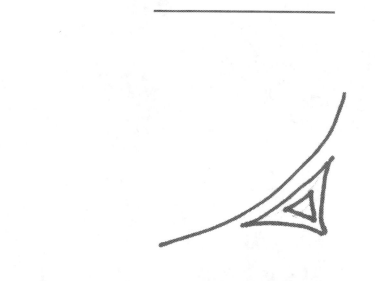

In his dreams, he watched himself as if from outside, like a shadow. He was sitting with Aparna, watching the India-England ODI. Kevin Pietersen, his favourite English player, was on fire. It was a series of seven ODI matches, and India had won the first four. The English team had their pride at stake. And the Indian team with their charismatic captain, Dhoni, was looking for a clean sweep.

Apu was fully attired. She looked beautiful in a check shirt and blue jeans, her long hair drawn into a knot at the back of her head. She sat close to him, not watching the match really. She wanted to go to Mama Mia!—the gelato ice cream shop close by and have an ice cream.

He had told her, 'Apu, your cab will be here any time soon. You have to catch that flight to Mumbai. Not today please, sweetheart. I promise, when you are back this weekend, I shall take you out for a gelato.' Before he could finish his sentence, the phone rang; the cab driver was already there.

'Apu, have you taken your boarding pass?'
'Sorry, forgot totally.'
Amit rushed into the study to pick up the boarding pass printout and handed it to her.

They would never get a chance to go for the ice cream. His shadowy self screamed at himself, 'Stop her! Do not let her go to Mumbai!' All in vain.

That was when he would wake up.

+ + + + + + + + + + + + + +

He woke up and drew the curtains. It was a gloomy winter morning in Calcutta. The sun had not risen, and the city was covered with fog. The beautiful view from his balcony was covered with a grey, gloomy veil. He pulled up the blanket and tried to go back to sleep. He tossed and turned and realised that it was useless. So many things were useless and meaningless nowadays. Just like his life.

There was nothing to look forward to—most importantly, no one to come back home to. Most of the days, he staggered back to his apartment late into the night; nevertheless, he still had to come to his apartment, which now was a painful reminder of what was and what could have been. His life was an incessant meaningless struggle of going through the grind, working too hard into late hours, missing meals, and missing all the good things that life offers you.

All he wanted to do, especially on this day, was to recoil into himself, making a perfect little comma, much like the way he was in the warm safety of his mother's womb, before he was born. He wanted to feel that warmth. Something he had not felt even for a moment in the last three long years. He tried to make sense of what had happened and why it had happened to him.

The doorbell rang. It was Mira, his morning attendant, though it would hardly be doing any justice calling her that, considering how long he had known Mira and what Mira had done for him.

+ + + + + + + + + + + + + + +

Amit was oblivious of the chilling cold and the cripplingly noxious smell. He was barely conscious, guided by people who looked sympathetically at his expensive attire.

He was still in the office suit he had worn to office yesterday. It was a gift from Apu.

And then he had spotted her. She was calm, as if sleeping, at peace with the world, her body still and cold; some of her curly, dishevelled hair was on her eyes. He had seen that so many times when he held her and stroked her hair softly as they lay in bed together. She was always the one to cuddle up to him. Whenever he pointed that out, she would roll her eyes in mock anger and cuddle up even more.

Amit desperately tried to call out to Apu loudly; only, there was no sound, just the dull thud as he fell on the hard floor. And that was when he became aware of the sharp antiseptic smell of the morgue. 'Is that how death smelt like?' he thought.

+ + + + + + + + + + + + + +

Mira was a single, unmarried mother; nobody knew who the father of her child was. Not even Gopal'da, Mira's father. In a conservative Bengali society, this can destroy a woman forever, not Mira. She had an amazing zest for life. She worked hard to bring up Durga—her daughter—but never ever mentioned who her father was, as if it was good enough to have a mother like Mira. She was always dressed in a white printed cotton sari and never wore any ornaments, except for a pair of gold earrings. It was as if she was in a perpetual mourning, yet her optimism was contagious. Mira was an enigma.

Mira was a nurse by profession, but she voluntarily prepared the morning tea for Amit. It was not because of the money; maybe it was because they had known each other from their childhood days, or maybe it was because Amit was the one to stand by her when the baby came unannounced, and she was ostracised by all. And maybe after Apu was not there, she never had the heart to leave Amit all alone. Every morning she would be there right at six o'clock and prepare the morning tea for Amit.

Mira actually started working for Amit when she came to know about her impending motherhood. She was all dishevelled and had come to her childhood friend Amit, seeking advice. It was 25 December 2007. Amit and Apu had planned to go for the Christmas lunch at Calcutta Club. Apu had opened the door for Mira.

'Amit, I needed to talk to you.'

'Yes, Mira.'

'Amit, since Ashok has passed away. You are my only friend.'

'Yes, Mira.' Amit had comforted Mira.

'Why don't you make yourself comfortable, Mira?'

She was panting for breath after walking up four flights of stairs.

'Would you like a cup of tea? Apu makes the best tea in the world.'

'OK, Amit,' she said as she stopped fidgeting with her fingers. It was almost as if she had resolved something in her mind.

It was after she had tea that she told Amit about her predicament.

'Amit, I am pregnant.'

'Oh!' Amit was stunned.

'Who's the father?' he wondered. 'Mira was so proud, so unreachable, who was it that dared to cross that bridge amongst his friends?' he wondered.

He himself had nurtured a soft corner for Mira since his childhood, but he could never muster enough courage to tell her about it. Then, as they grew up, given their difference in social status, they had drifted apart. He had often wondered that if they had been from the same social background, would he have had some chance with Mira.

'Amit, you know how my father is. He can be really stern. But I have to keep this baby, Amit.'

'OK, who is the father, Mira? Let us talk to the father, and Gopal'da would accept everything.'

'I cannot, Amit.'

'Why not, Mira?'

'I cannot, Amit.'

'I want to keep it. And anyways, it is too late for that.'

At this point, Apu sat down beside Mira. She held Mira's hands.

Mira looked up. 'Amit I need financial support for a couple of months till I finish my nursing course and get a decent job.'

'Do not worry, Mira,' Apu replied in lieu of Amit.

Apu used to always do this. She treated Amit's friends as hers, Amit's family as her own, and whenever Amit found himself in a tight corner, every time she would somehow come to his rescue like mother goddess 'Durga'—the invincible one.

Mira looked up. 'But I do not want to take money from my childhood friend. I can work for you though.'

Apu exchanged a glance with Amit. Amit was a little reluctant. Not sure how his fiancée would take the request of his childhood friend.

It was Apu who took Mira to the kitchen and told her, 'Can you make tea for us, every morning?'

Mira stared at Apu with disbelief.

Apu added hastily, 'Neither of us wants to get up and prepare the morning tea. Also you know, I have this special way of making it, which I learnt from my mother.' Apu continued, 'It is not something you can teach a maid.'

By this time, Mira was trying hard to conceal her tears and smile at Apu's desperate attempt to prove that they needed her for making their morning tea.

'Yes, Apu, I would gladly do it.' Mira held Apu's hand in gratitude.

Mira added 'And I will never forget how my best friend's fiancée saved my child.'

They had become instant friends—Apu and Mira. Unlike Apu, his friendship with Mira had always been a very unequal friendship, which had only got complicated over the years due to the difference in their social statures and Amit's dormant attraction towards Mira.

Yet Amit only remembered being helped and comforted by Mira when he had nobody to turn to in his deepest and darkest hours. There was no way he could forget that. With all the newspapers churning out gory details every day and all those exclusive photos, it was impossible to forget.

+ + + + + + + + + + + + + + +

Amit's train of thought was broken by Mira's voice.

'Amit, why don't you put on a jacket take a seat? I will quickly get your hot cup of tea. It is very cold today.'

Amit loved the morning fresh tea that Mira prepared. She had learnt it from Apu. It somehow gave him a strange consolation that Apu was still around. As Amit looked out of his balcony into the bleak, foggy day, he sipped his morning elixir. The aroma spread through his senses, rejuvenating him, reminding him of days when life meant something. He wondered if he would have cared to get up without the promise of hot, refreshing morning tea and the warm smile from Mira. Even now, even in his darkest hour, Mira always made Amit realise that there was still a reason to smile.

+ + + + + + + + + + + + + +

Amit had known Mira since his childhood days. In the Hindustan Road *para*, all the kids used to play together in the field. All the children, right from the kids of big businessmen to the tea vendor's daughter, used to hang out together. In fact, in the social paradigm of *para* kids club, Mira was much ahead of Amit, in spite of their apparent class difference. Mira's father had a tea and cake stall which used to dish out *singharas*—a delicious dish with cauliflower and potatoes rolled into a triangular-shaped Bengali white wheat dumpling. The additional attraction of having her in their team was the occasional treat of delicious *singharas* from the lovely daughter of Gopal'da. Amit had no such social advantages at that age, being the only son of a manager of a manufacturing company. Mira was actually Amit's first girlfriend in the sense that she was a friend who was a girl too. The other friend was Ashok. Even in their group, Ashok, Amit, and Mira had something like a secret society of three. They were the 'three musketeers'. They even took an oath that three of them would always protect each other. And if one of them was in trouble, the other two would extend unquestioned allegiance.

During his adolescence years, Amit had developed a huge crush on Mira. But nothing ever materialised as Amit never said anything. He was afraid of losing Mira as a friend.

Actually, he was afraid of losing Mira and Ashok. They were like his insurance in a strange way. There were perhaps the only real friends that he made in his childhood, and he knew they would always be there for him, come what may.

They had lost Ashok in a freak accident in December 2007. Ashok was settling well as a pantry staff in the railways. The pay was good for him. It happened at Nijbari near New Jalpaiguri in North Bengal. All that the newspapers said was '4055 down Brahmaputra Mail was derailed'. Most newspapers did not even report it.

Amit did not want to lose Mira. Possibly he was, in a way, subconsciously honouring that secret pact that they had taken to protect each other. After all, since Amit was the lankiest of them all, Ashok and Mira had always protected Amit from other bullies.

+ + + + + + + + + + + + + + +

Amit hated November now. But it had not been like this always. There was a time when life was a song and Amit loved Calcutta winters. He famously told his friends that he was not open for any on-site assignment from September to January. Amit then was the optimistic, enthusiastic person who could turn all negative things into positive with his Midas touch. Everything was on a song.

He remembered the day Apu had moved in with him. She had dropped in with a suitcase and a couple of her regular dresses, her laptop, and her iPod. 'Everything else,' she had said, 'will take care of itself.' When he opened the door and found Apu at his doorsteps, he possibly must have looked strangely at Apu, with a lot of consternation.

'Sorry, Amit, could not put with my aunt any more. She absolutely hates you.'

Amit had nodded his head and carried her suitcase into his apartment, as if in a trance.

'Don't worry, we can share the rent 50:50.'

And then in a deep voice she had said, 'Don't worry, Amit, I will never be a burden on you. I would rather move out, if it is uncomfortable for you.'

That was the first time Amit had kissed Apu. Apu never moved out.

Amit remember every little detail about Apu—her eyes, the way she looked at him, the way she turned speechless every time he held her tight, her *kajol* (which would always darken her eyelids), and the mole just between her cheekbones and her nose. He mostly remembered her smell, sweet and earthy, a little like the smell of raindrops on a hot summer afternoon.

+ + + + + + + + + + + + + +

It was a winter in Calcutta. His ailing mother had called him from Siliguri a day before that fateful night.

'Amit, your mother here.'

'Yes, Mother.'

'Amit, I am looking at a date for engagement in the auspicious month of Magh' (sometime in mid-January).

'It will be a good time to get married.'

Amit could visualise his mother with her *panjika*—a pink book with black pictures depicting each star

135

shine, typically used to fix up auspicious times like marriages, housewarmings, etc. His mother used to always refer to this 'Beni Madhav Seal *Panjika*' for any auspicious function. He knew that his mother, though a liberal-minded person, wanted him and Apu to get married as soon as possible.

He specially cherished the time that they used spend together in the mornings. Apu was an early riser.

'Apu, where you going?' Amit would mumble in his sleep.

'It is six o'clock, Amit. I am getting up.'

'No, please.'

'Sorry?'

'It is only six, and today is a holiday. I want to hold you tight and sleep in your arms.'

'Amit . . .'

'Hmmmm . . . Apu . . . please,' he would mumble. 'Please run your fingers through my hair and make me go to sleep.'

'OK, *baba,* I will invite all the angels of sleep.'

Apu would run her fingers through his hair, and Amit would indulge in her sweet smell as they laid together, oblivious of time. The sun would peek through the curtain and play light and shadow across Apu's soft features.

That day it was even more special. He was imagining Apu as his bride.

'Apu, Ma had called.'

'Oh! How is she? When is she coming to visit?'

'Apu, she wants to fix up a date in winter itself.'

'Date? What for?'

'She wants her son to marry and get settled.'

Apu did not reply. She was still.

'So she wanted to know if Miss Aparna Pal would be OK with a January date.'

It finally registered. Apu was practically over the moon. Apu and he held hands, as they sipped tea in the balcony overlooking the terrace.

Apu used to make tea in the old traditional way with tea leaves in an earthen pot. She used to say that tea never tastes the same with tea bags. She had this strange concoction that she made with cinnamon, honey, and bay leaves that she used to call 'the magic formula'. The tea used to smell like heaven. Apu had got Amit hooked on her tea like an addict. Amit would declare in mock anger that he was definitely going to take her tea mixture for drug testing. It was as irresistible and soothing as Apu herself. Apu had once said that sipping that tea was like coming back home. She could not have been more right.

Apu was a strange person; she was optimistic to the hilt, yet she used to have her moments of insecurity like when meeting Amit's mother for the first time. She was fiercely intelligent and aggressive, and yet there was this strange laziness about her. Amit used to occasionally tell her that she would make a great housewife. Apu used to threaten him, 'You never know, Amit, I might just decide to quit everything and be dependent on you.' In spite of all her sharpness and all the effort she put in her work, she was, in a peculiar way, not ambitious.

Apu had a flight to catch that day. It was a meeting with her boss in Mumbai, due after her winning over one of the largest retail clients from Citibank. Apu had put up months of effort to bag the prize catch, but after that she was very nonchalant about it. This was a meeting that she had dreamt about the last two years, but when it came to it, Apu seemed uninterested.

She told Amit, 'It is such a wonderful day. I do not feel like catching the afternoon flight and be in Mumbai.'

'Apu, don't be a spoilsport. You keep on complaining about your boss, and now that he wants to appreciate you, you cannot just cancel your trip.'

Apu protested, 'It is such a wonderful day, Amit. I just want to be with you.'

If only Amit had listened to Apu and not prodded her. If, only.

'Apu, you will be back at the weekend, and anyways, I also have to go to office today. The customer is visiting our facilities today. I cannot take off. But I promise you, we will laze the whole weekend, on the twenty-ninth and thirtieth,' he had said.

Little did Amit know that he would be at Mumbai on the weekend of 29 and 30 November; only, Apu would not be with him, not in the way he wanted her to be. It was 2011 now. It was three years now. It was exactly the same day, three years back.

+ + + + + + + + + + + + + + +

Apu wondered if he should tell Mira that he had put up his flat for sale. He did not know any more what he wanted from life.

Mira was sipping her tea and looking oddly at her childhood friend. She said, 'Amit, it is a Saturday this year, a weekend. I do not want you to be alone at home on this date.'

'Mira, I was not the only one who lost. I would rather be left alone on this day, Mira.'

Mira took a deep breath and said, 'Remember, you always wanted to go to our home at Hoogly?'

Amit said, 'No, I have been there.'

Mira replied, 'That was years back, Amit. We were kids.'

Amit answered, 'Yes, long time back.'

Mira continued, 'Amit, would you, for once, heed a request?'

Amit said, 'You know, Mira, I would. Tell me.'

Mira continued, 'Don't stay back, Amit. Come with me. I am going home today to be with Durga for the weekend. It will be good if you can come.' Durga was Mira's daughter.

After a long moment of silence Amit said, 'OK, Mira. I shall come.'

Amit was strangely relieved that he did not have to stay back at their apartment, surrounded by Apu's memories, on this date. But he did not believe that he could escape the pain and the guilt by just being away.

+ + + + + + + + + + + + + +

They reached Mira's father's place at Hoogly, almost in the afternoon.

Durga came running to her mother. Durga was now almost four years old. Durga reminded Amit of Mira in her childhood, carefree days.

Gopal'da, Mira's father, was very surprised to see Amit. He said, 'Amit, what a pleasant surprise. So how are you?'

They had lentils, vegetables, and fish curry. The ingredients were fresh, and it was cooked well, much better than his office canteen.

Later, as Mira got busy with Durga, Gopal'da told him sadly that he worried about Mira.

'Mira is my only daughter, Amit. Look after Mira when I am no more. Will you, Amit?'

'Yes, *Mesomasai* (uncle). I will try.'

'You are her only friend.'

He lamented that Mira was determined not to get married again.

Later in the evening as Amit sat on the river bank, his mind went back to that fateful night in November.

He remembered Leopold Café; it really was Leopold Coffee and Bar. It was pretty much the quintessential tourist eatery where wannabe literary types came in the hope of scoping their hero. He tried to think of Apu at the café, which used to be normally noisy and rather smoky. 'Was Apu having crispy chilly chicken with chilled beer at her favourite joint, blissfully unaware of the heinous gunmen? Did she die instantly, or was it painful? Why couldn't she duck? She could have at least tried to save herself. Was she so absorbed in her dreams of setting up a home with Amit that she had not even noticed the strange fellows, before they started firing?'

Amit had thought this again and again. He had cried at night thinking if only he had not prodded Apu to go to Mumbai that day. He had dreamt several nights that lackadaisical as Apu was, she had missed the Mumbai flight, in spite of Amit prodding her, and had stayed back. That 26 November 2008 never happened. It was only a big bad nightmare.

As Amit stared at the still water of Ganges, he wanted to feel the Ganges. He did not know how to swim; that's why he never ventured out in the water. But something possessed him, and he slowly went down the ghat. He was almost neck deep in water, lost in a different world, when strangely he heard the voice of Mira from his childhood days crying out at him. Ashok was right there beside her.

Suddenly Amit woke up from the trance and realised that it was Durga calling out at him loudly from the bank.

She called, 'Mitma, Mitma!' She could not pronounce 'Amit *mama*' (uncle) hence the short cut 'Mitma'.

And as he gathered himself slowly, a sudden warmth spread through his heart, a feeling he had not felt even for a moment in the last three desolate years. He also realised why Durga looked so familiar and who Durga's father was.

He went back to the bank, all drenched. As water dripped from him, he picked up Durga and wrapped her in his arms. Once again he felt that warmth spread in his heart in the cold winter evening by the Ganges. Mira rushed out with a towel as soon as she saw Amit and Durga.

She said, 'Oh my! Look how wet you are! Let me make you two a warm cup of tea, and please get in. It is getting late. Don't stay outside any more. Get in, Amit.'

Amit held Durga close to his heart, and as he sipped his tea, he knew he was finally home.

My King's Palace

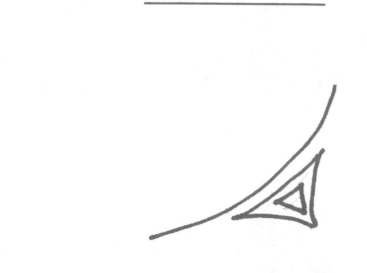

If anyone came to know about my king's palace, I fear it would vanish into thin air. If any world-weary traveller ventured across this remote stretch on the earth's surface, this haven of happiness where imperfection reflects the individual pieces of glass in the kaleidoscopic view of life, then perhaps he would have nothing to say but his soul would not be speechless.

On a night as cloudy as this, when infants dreamt under the shelter of the mighty sky and occasionally the leaves of the trees rustled and the droning cicadas sang overtures to the rain, the girl crossed over. The final words of the last chapter of her late father's diary:

> My daughter has taken the cage of darkness in my heart and set it free. She has given me a reason to live and a reason to smile. For the first time in my life, my shoulders have served a purpose. I cannot thank the Lord enough for bringing her in my arms. She has always been there with me through my hard times and, quite to the contrary, has wiped my tears away before any came in her eyes. There are trials and rewards throughout one's life, and I hope that I will be able to be there for my daughter for as long as

she needs me and forever. And Katie, 'If kisses were snowflakes, I'd send you a blizzard.'

Love Now and Always
Dad

There that night as hope lay shredded and she sobbed hard and long, the tears inundating her eyes blurring the vision of the world, she prayed to the Lord to bring back her father, knowing full well that the grains of sand which had slipped from her hands were lost forever.

As she lay curled up next to the couch where she and her father had spent numerous hours together, she remembered the season of summer, the season of growth and rejoices. Her heart gleamed with the fresh new fruits in bloom, and she dreamt about her father—how he would lift her high, almost touching the tree with its head reaching for the sky; his hand encasing hers, telling her everything would be all right. She dreamt how tall she could be on her father's shoulder, but most of all she dreamt of those chilly nights of winters when the cold winds knew no boundaries. Then the daughter and the father, the king and his little princess, would snuggle close to each other under an old blanket with holes, perhaps because the mites had eaten it away. Together they would imagine the possibilities of aliens in space or of flying unicorns in the upstairs attic or a shiny silver penny left by the tooth fairy that would bring wealth and prosperity to their little world and make some of their dreams come true.

The clock chimed too many times, and thoughts tick-tocked in her mind. Questions collided, memories enlivened, the future appeared in front of her eyes. The road appeared dusty and 'well-worn'. It had puddles, leaves, and the dry pavement. Forgotten words. Fragile promises and futile efforts. A flood of possibilities somersaulted in her head.

Cloaked in grief, she walked the streets, searching for something invisible. The silence of the night was left undisturbed, until it was broken by her heavy footsteps and deep breaths. The vicinity stuck by its promise, remaining silent.

'She looked down the memory lane looking for the last words, the last memories, the idle hours she had spent together with her father, the shards of promises and myths of premonitions called happiness. Then she stumbled upon a stranger, a contradictory word, an old friend—courage.'

The first of the monsoon showers darkened patches of the parched earth. Her father would have lifted her up and made sure that she did not wet her feet. Scared, afraid, and wet she crossed over . . . to the one place on the earth where a father became his daughter's first love, where you could feel that it was easy to be a man, a husband, but it took something more to be a father; where poverty and isolation was numbed silent under the euphonic articulations of laughter's lasting vibrations. That is where a man became a father, a father became a king and lived forever—'My king's palace.'

It was her sanctuary. Her own. And she knew that her father was waiting for her there. She smiled, after a long time.